TRIP WALK

TRIP WALK

C.M. HALSTEAD

TRIP WALK
BOOK ONE OF THE TRIPPER SERIES

Cover and Interior design by Ted Ruybal
Manufactured in the United States of America

For more information, please contact:

Wisdom House Books
www.wisdomhousebooks.com

Paperback ISBN 13: 978-0-9863445-1-0
Hard Case ISBN 13: 978-0-9863445-0-3
E-Book ISBN 13: 978-0-9863445-2-7

LCCN: 2015902351

FICTION / Science Fiction / Time Travel / Adventure
1 2 3 4 5 6 7 8 9 10

DEDICATION

To my wife Tonya,
for teaching me what support looks like.

CONTENTS

INTRODUCTION

PHILOSOPHY OF TIME TRAVEL: THOUGHTS AND FEASIBILITY

What concerns me most is not whether or not time travel is feasible, but rather what human kind will do with it once it figures out how to make it happen.

That is, if it has not already; for all human kind needs to accomplish a goal is to determine its importance.

As soon as we deem something important, we figure out how to make it happen. Prime examples of this are landing on the moon, swimming the English Channel, hiking around the world, or jumping from near space and landing on earth by parachute. As Felix Baumgartner said, "The only thing standing between you and your goal, is the bullshit story you keep telling yourself as to why you can't achieve it." Felix Baumgartner is an Austrian skydiver and daredevil, who in 2012 was the first human

to break the sound barrier without powered assistance. He accomplished this purely with his body and gravity. Jumping from a helium balloon floating 5 1/2 miles above the earth's surface, he accelerated to a top speed of 843 miles per hour, purely because he had the idea to do so. Even he had to overcome fears to accomplish his goal; we all do.

The only thing that keeps us from accomplishing anything is fear; fear of change, fear of failure, fear of something or someone different, fear of success even (seems strange, yet this seems to exist in most people, in some way, shape, or form).

I believe it is this fear that prevails in the mind of those most resistant to time travel. Who wants to believe that life as it exists can be changed by someone other than ourselves? Who wants to believe that you can go back in time and do things to change my now? Damn! I like my life, you can't go back and steal my girl or shoot my parents . . . anything good or bad to change where I am now. Unless of course I hate my now, then please, by all means, go back in time and fix it. Just make sure you fix it to my advantage or my version of it.

Humans throughout documented history have taken the same actions for and against each other since the beginning of time. Going back in time will not change these behaviors, just the game of life. The rules would change; it would not be once and final. One could go back and do it differently the second time. Better or worse, since humans are the same now as then, just with different technology, it will still be a world of flux, battles of good and bad, all still relative to your perspective and which side of the street you are standing on.

Same battle, different rules.

Time travel means we can fight the same fight over and over in the same period of time as opposed to fighting different battles the same way, as time travels.

Again; who's to say time travel doesn't already exist. People are just afraid of it . . . and fear is the mind killer, the erasure of thought and reason. Fear institutes flight, fight or freeze; that part of the brain is not made to think or rationalize, rather to react without thought.

Thought is brought on by a desire to accomplish something, a goal or challenge: thought finishes books, builds skyscrapers and allows the possibility of time travel.

Who knows, you may be reading this while on your sub-orbital space ride with the space tourism industry; although looking out the window and contemplating it all might be a better idea.

Enjoy the ride.

CHAPTER ONE

The Technician readies the room. He is one of the few who knows what for . . . knows that there will soon be troops with guns, high end VIPs; not to mention the tops of all the Super Powers surely watching secretly from above. They were all informed that this launch would be different, different because there is a changing of the guard coming—a new boss arrives today! It is actually exciting to Loren. He doesn't like this current boss. There is something funky and stinky about him. So slick, nothing sticks . . . and that suit!

Finishing up he grabs his bag and rushes to catch up with his favorite girl. She is on lunch, and he knows it is his last chance to see her before all the craziness begins; 24-36 hours this one is scheduled to take. He has been at this long enough to know that is an accurate estimate and that's IF everything goes right. Two launches ago, someone lost it, or should I say, figured out what was up. Having apparently been sold a bill of goods as to what was about to happen or possibly not been given a choice, he decided to make a different choice. A big, burly Cajun, about twice as wide as he was front to back, Loren remembers wondering if he could scratch his back. Regardless, Loren was pretty sure based on his demeanor and facial expression that the guy would just grab the nearest person and force him to scratch the middle of his back. (Loren remembers the image that went through his head at the time—the big dude grabbing a skinny girl by the ankles and using her to scratch his back, sound effects and everything, *ert ur, ert ur.*)

Walking to the door, he reaches to push it outward but it opens a few inches before his hand. As he keeps walking forward, his hand just won't catch up to the door. It's at this point that he realizes someone is opening the door from outside the room. He looks up and sees oxford shoes and then that suit; it is his boss, briefcase in hand as always, and a military man with a chest full of fruit salad is walking next to him. Medals galore adorn his chest, actually an easy feat in this age of war. All a trooper has to do is live long enough and his uniform will fill with medals. The key words there are: live long enough . . .

Loren excuses himself and holds the door for the brief second it takes the two men to walk through. Lost in conversation, they merely nod their thanks in his general direction. Continuing on his current mission, Loren walks down the hall to find his girl. He lets his thoughts wander as he searches.

This is Loren's first time as head scientist for a project. He is hoping this one will be a success. They already know the last few were mostly failures. The results appear in the computers relatively quickly in the present time, a matter of hours in the most complicated scenarios. Not so for the poor souls sent to handle things, to change things and make them right, or at least our version of right. Loren secretly wonders if he will rot in hell. Because he practices the ancient Christian religion (Southern Baptist by upbringing), he still manages to hold onto a lot of the beliefs. . .it's hard not to when they were beaten into you from an early age until you managed to leave home. Even then, the fear of hell is there, well that, and the love of the music. Nothing gets a body pumping like the Southern Baptists do with their hymns. . .they get so fired up, an EMT is required to attend just to handle the rapid heartbeats and concussions from heads hitting the ground when they pass out from divine intervention, or lack of oxygen, whichever comes first.

Loren forces himself back to the present.

Pushing the hymns from his lips and back into his brain, he refocuses his eyes on the checklist in his hand. He has checked it more than Santa would already, double in fact and is checking it just one more time just in case. All items are checked; he scans it again. Yep, all items still checked. Looking around, seeking something else to distract himself with, he finds her nowhere at all. After checking all the usual haunts, he decides to join the rest of the crew at the lunchroom. Time to grab one more giant meal before the marathon of watching panels, making adjustments and decisions, and hoping nothing fails. It's no wonder lead technicians are only allowed to head two of these in a row "I am stressed as hell," Loren thinks to himself.

"Oops, sorry, Mom," Loren says out loud as if she could still hear his thoughts. Even in death he is pretty sure she is keeping tabs on him. She always did.

CHAPTER TWO

The two men walk with intention into the Operations room, barely missing a tech on his way out. The Ops tech was obviously in a hurry as are most people in this general area at the moment. Even though they have done this before, quite a few times in fact, there is always that busy bee, nervous type of energy to deal with prior to a mission.

The man in the suit appears to be bringing the military man up to speed. "The fun of these events is that anything can happen, anything at all; from catastrophic equipment failure to that big, burly S.O.B. from Louisiana who about took everybody out when he freaked out. Stopping that big Cajun was a bitch and one hell of a loss. We needed him for the mission, needed him bad, needed him for that very reason he was trying to escape. That big, burly Cajun would take on anybody at any time, and

that is exactly what was needed to take on his part of that mission. It wasn't the most pivotal part of that mission, but he was still needed for it to succeed as planned."

The man in the suit is moving on to be the head of the International Spy division (affectionately known as I.S. because it just "is"). One would never know it from looking at him. He just looks like a 1980s Wall Street mogul in his high sheen, woven suit; an interesting style for someone residing in the year 2114. His hair is perfectly gelled and feathered back. The gel in his hair provides a Superman-like, blue sheen to his jet black hair. This man has even gone all out and had some leather oxford shoes made for himself, which he keeps in perfect condition, and I mean perfect.

The other man's appearance is just as perfect, albeit the military version, from shiny shoes to the immaculate head cover (held with the perfect amount of pressure) between his arm and his side. Not a fingerprint can be seen on its brim even though he isn't wearing gloves. All seams line up in a perfect gig line, a perfect straight line from jacket top, to the crotch of the pants. There are only four creases in the entire uniform; the two running down the pant legs and the two in the back of the jacket, no other lines, creases, wrinkles or wear marks of any kind. It is as if he had floated to this present location instead of just arriving after a day of travel. It is obvious he spent

as much time on his uniform as the spy did on his suits.

Having only met the spy a few moments ago, Colonel Petzer is subtly sizing him up. It is the man's attention to detail that gives him away, his personality that is. There are no tailors, no maids, and no known way to get a suit like that; yet, this man has an immaculately tailored suit with no Irish pennants, which are pieces of thread that poke out from the seams on an item of clothing. These always seem to appear out of nowhere and at random times from every item of clothing ever made. It takes an almost constant vigilance to keep anything free and clear of Irish pennants, and this man had none. "I would know." Colonel Petzer thinks to himself. Having 25 years as an officer under his belt, and most of those years as an inquisitor during the inspections, he could pick out an Irish pennant with his eye two ranks back. He would keep an eye on it once he had spotted it. He at times would even make a comment before he got there and give them a chance to handle it if they could. If they did he would automatically pass them on inspection! I mean if a trooper can find a way to cut off a piece of string while standing in formation at attention, with three officers walking through the ranks, eyeballing every action the troopers made, that told the colonel several things: he was prepared, he had a knife in his pocket even at inspections, and he was smooth, swift, and smart, which

easily translates to Swift, Silent, and Deadly—what each elite trooper desires to be. That takes precedence over an Irish pennant that could have snuck its sneaky ass out from the seams on the march between quarters and the grinder any day.

Speaking, Andrew Roberts brings him back to the present. "You ok, Colonel?"

"Yes, perfectly fine, Mr. Roberts. Just reminiscing a bit in my mind," he replies.

The two are standing in the Operations room because they figure it is the best place to have this kind of conversation. Mr. Roberts knows that around here, right before a mission, the only room that isn't occupied is the room in which the activity is about to happen. Everyone is about to spend a tremendous amount of time in this large, electronics filled room. The room even has a few bathrooms with showers, a full kitchen with stocked fridge, and cupboards. All personnel want to be anywhere but here while they can be. After all, once the green light goes on, nobody leaves or enters what becomes "Operations Control" or O.C. to most.

"So what are the need to knows?" the Colonel asks of Mr. Roberts.

"The particulars are still coming together on this group. It might be best to read the briefs on them. This team has three new members because of recent restructuring and that incident we briefly talked about," Andrew gestures to a table nearby, "Shall we sit?"

As they both situate themselves he continues, "One of the members just received a promotion as well, so there are three rookies on this mission, always a variable."

He places his titanium case onto the table. Putting three fingers from his left hand and two from his right onto the case, the case opens, almost like magic. The fingerprint case is of spy legend; long ago it became a standard issue item for the Spy Corps. At first it seemed like it would be anti-productive. Many a spy had their fingers cut off while bad guys attempted to get into the particulars of the spy's carry case. In spite of several years of bad guy failure, it took a while for the world to accept that unless you apply the fingers in the proper order, and from a live hand, then and only then will the case open like magic. In the meantime the I.S. surgeons became experts at reattaching fingers. Rumor has it; many became rich after leaving the corps by replacing fingers on the black market. The only way to start anew these days is with new fingerprints!

Mr. Roberts pulls a stack of files from his carry case. Secretly loving the old-school feel of files and papers, he revels in the fact that only a few copies of these files exist. There is no soft data, no computer records of the contents of these files. Heck, the people in the files were

about to be removed from all soft data computer files through time, if not expunged from digital existence already. There will soon be a computer bot and worms set free on the net looking for any piece of evidence of the existence of their particular birth-given name. There will be no Fred Smith or Jane Doe, or whatever their name is, in computer existence within 48 hours (72 max, his brain corrects him) tops. "How would you like to do this, Colonel Petzer?"

The Colonel reaches for the top file. "How about I glance through them one by one and you can tell me what you know about each one as I read through them? I will ask any questions that arise while we are going through. Sound good, Mr. Roberts?"

"You can call me Andrew, Colonel," he says matter-of-factly. "We are going to be on this project for longer than we know. Might as well be relaxed with each other."

The Colonel releases an under the breath, exhaling laugh, knowing exactly what Mr. Roberts, was talking about.

"Sounds good, Andrew. You can call me Colonel. It's been so long, even I don't remember my first name," the Colonel bemuses.

Smiling, Andrew says, "I heard you had one hell of a nickname though."

The Colonel outright belly laughs, opening the first file and saying, "Yes, yes, I do."

Colonel Petzer distracts, wanting to save that story for later. "Ok, how about this guy?" He glances down the first page, skimming through the paragraphs and then looks up at the picture. "Or girl?" he says more at his assumption than his surprise.

Mr. Roberts glances across the table and sees the picture, "Ah yes, that one's a pistol."

The Colonel reads the jacket. "Rosa Fernandez, former Marine turned SWAT team member."

"She was good enough and stuck at it long enough to become the first female SWAT Captain. She was leading one of Chicago's finest divisions until it all hit the fan and we snagged her." Mr. Roberts offers up.

The Colonel, reading on, states, "You snagged her in 2012? How long has she been at this for us Andrew . . . and how?"

"She has been with us for four years now." he replies.

"But this is 2114." Petzer states as a matter of fact.

Andrew Roberts take a deep breath. "Yep, so this is the need to know part that you now get to know." Making direct eye contact with the Colonel he continues, "We have been taking specialists and experts from different time frames. We have found a way to factor in risk, life situations, and emotional status into our computer bots. They rove around and gather data, and when it gets back to us we sort through it for things that fit. And when

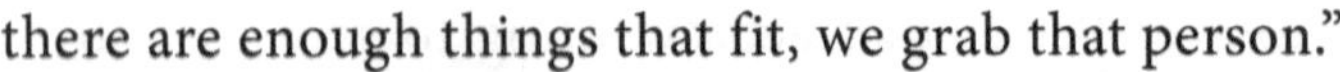

there are enough things that fit, we grab that person."

"Grab, not ask or buy them?" Colonel Petzer questions.

"Well it depends; some are given more choice than others. Some are "counseled" into doing it, which can take years. It all depends on their personality traits and their situation. We are, in most cases, trying to make them think it was their idea." Mr Roberts starts laughing. "Kinda like dealing with my ex! It just works better that way."

The Colonel takes a moment to let it all sink in. He received several briefings before committing to his new position as division head of this project. He'd been told about time travel and missions to change the past and how important this project is to the future of their current way of life. Yet it still has not hit home. I mean, how could it? There is still this part of him that thinks this is all a joke and he is waiting for the Generals to come bursting forth laughing and saying, "Gotcha!" Yet things just keep moving forward. No reality show producers or crews appear with their high tech cameras. No laughing Generals. The pinches he applies to the back of his left hand continue to be felt. So he moves on. "Ok, next is?"

CHAPTER THREE

Loren walks into the dining area; the room is pretty full and usually is just before mission start. We all have the same desire to consume sustenance before a long day. Food, and probably just as important, connection and stress relief can be found here. From the sounds in the room, there is plenty of it being consumed here.

He can hear a joke being told just off to his left. The body language around the table shows that all are at peak interest to the joke being told, most leaning in and listening intently. A few are eating while listening, but most have at least paused mid feed to hear what is coming. The joke teller, thriving on the audience, builds his story to a crescendo. Loren stops to half-heartedly listen in. "Fifty dollars is fifty dollars," he hears from afar. The table erupts in groans and laughter; a little food even falls off the forks of those who insisted on eating throughout the joke. Must've been a good one based on the reactions.

As Loren walks away he slowly pans his head back and forth looking for his girl. She was usually easy to spot. That curly red hair stood out in a crowd, especially one full of mostly lab coats, overalls, grey suits, and military style clothing. Looking around, he doesn't see her. "Huh," he thinks to himself. Loren had naturally assumed she would be here. After all, everybody is here. Scanning one more time his eyes fall on one big empty table. Well, except for them of course. Doh! What is he thinking? The Trippers don't come in to eat until we all are gone, back to our posts, doing final checks. A crazy thought runs through his head. "Nah," he thinks. She would've told him. She could be though; she could totally be a Tripper!

Walking straight through the dining hall, he walks out the other side headed for dorm row. A long row of hallways leading to all the dorm and housing wings ran off the north side of the complex. Loren is thinking maybe she is trying to surprise him in his room. He went there every day during his lunch. Nothing like a ten minute nap to get one through the afternoon, followed by gratuitous espresso, of course.

Arriving at 4C Loren opens his suite door. Peeking in as he enters, he half expects to smell her. He doesn't

. . . well, maybe faintly. Intriguing. Walking in anyway, he goes to his bunk room, nothing. He looks in the bathroom, nothing. And just in case, he checks the balcony overlooking the common area below. Living totally underground, the common area is the closest to an outside park, a big expanse of sports courts and grass and even a pond. Loren thinks, "It's amazing how they can keep this shit alive so far under the ground. Technology, you gotta love it."

Actually Loren does. He's a Techie for sure. But where is his girl? Walking back into his quarters, he scans the room, and then he sees it. It is attached to the refrigerator unit with a magnet—a red envelope, his name written on the outside, a silver ink of sorts. Walking straight at it in a trancelike state, he bumps a table corner, hard. Barely noticing, he leans into it and pushes it out of the way slightly, so he could resume his course for the envelope. As he approaches it, he reaches out to it. Long before he gets to it, his hand is ready to receive. When he gets close enough, Loren pulls the red envelope off the fridge sending the magnet careening along the cupboard edges and onto the counter. The magnet stops its sudden unexpected journey by attaching itself to the toaster unit sitting on the counter. The magnet saves itself from the fate of falling between the counter and the oven where it would've attached itself to the side, never to be seen again.

Pulling open the envelope, hoping beyond all hope that he will be reading a good luck and congrats message, he knew beyond all doubt that that is just optimistic bullshit! Loren can now tell that something is up. All the signs of the last couple of weeks are flying through his brain one image at a time: how distant she's been, the mysterious late night visits with early morning departures for "extra duty" instead of staying for breakfast, the bruises, the strange smells on her—almost gunpowder, perfume and sulfur scents mixed together.

As all these thoughts run through his head he pulls open the envelope, slides out a card of the same red as the envelope and opens its contents. "My love, my dearest love, it is with great regret that I have to inform you of the termination of our relationship. Although our time together has been lovely, I must depart for times unknown." Loren's eyes widen as he reads the lines.

"No f-ing shit," comes out of his mouth in amazement. "No f-ing shit!" a little louder this time. After reading the signature "Love, June" this time he yells at the top of his lungs, "REALLY!!" The standard form of her note makes it abundantly clear that he has just been dumped by a Tripper. His body stands a little taller. Loren can feel his body filling with joy, elation even. "I mean, fuck," he thinks. I've been fucking a Tripper. It is a hope and a dream of all Techs to grab the attention of a Tripper, if

only for a little while. After all, they are the elite of the elite, the guardians of the future and of the now.

Putting the note down on the table as he hover-crafts his body over to the balcony, he takes a couple deep breaths and shouts, "I got to fuck a Tripper!" It echoes across the common area and bounces back at him. He listens, getting to hear that voice, his voice, with teenage-like joy in it, bouncing back at him. The joy and happiness at being dumped surpass his absorption at the moment. He is just too damn happy he managed to gain a connection with someone who is going to change the world—whether she knows it or not.

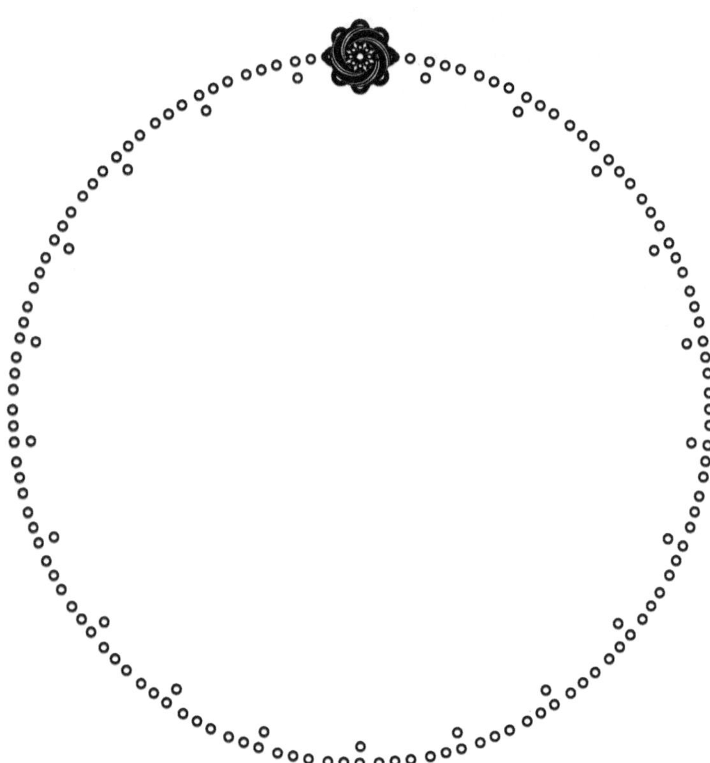

CHAPTER FOUR

John is not even trying to listen at this point. Listening to the final brief would just be a waste of his time. Dreaming about anything else is way more productive; since the beginning of the two-hour brief he has day-dreamt about that trip to Cancun with his long time high school friend. He thought for sure the trip would be his failsafe for closing the deal with her. He could have sworn she was showing signs of falling for him. Yah, he knew she was a lipstick lesbian, but still. She let him zip her up, watch her change. He was like a brother to her was the last thing she cried to him as she was leaving for the airport. He thinks "Oops, I really F'd that one up." F'd was his favorite word, new fav he should say. He had picked it up from the Hispanic tough girl a few months back when he had asked her if she would be his Latin lover for the duration of mission planning. John explained he could not continue being with her once the mission started but would enjoy frolicking with her prior to. He rubs his jaw remembering her succinct response. Even John takes an uppercut as a "no."

He glances over at the woman sitting next to him. They are both rookies to the team, the two of them; both recruited recently and still learning the ropes of their new profession. Brought in at the same time, they have spent the last six months together and are starting to know each other fairly well.

"The answer is no." June says to John without looking at him.

"No to what?"

"No, I will not be your redheaded Latin lover." John turns red. Damn, how did she know?

"And I am Irish," she says as she glances at him with that knowing look. Needing him to get it now! There is no way, ever. Even if she wasn't kinda in love with that skinny little lab tech. Even if they didn't work together. Even if the aliens were coming and the world was going to end. Even if he were the last man on the planet. She wonders how someone who has his build and look, has the impression that he is a ladies' man.

John knows he is not like the quiet, little lab rat she has spent her precious little spare time with. But still, you never know till you test the waters, just have to be smart enough to pull out when it gets rough.

Looking across the table at Rosa, he sees her give June a knowing look. Thinking to himself, "Note to self, John, women communicate amongst each other. Will have to be more careful in the future." How could she know the exact moment he was getting ready to ask her that? Was she psychic or something?

John looks around at the other six people sitting at the table. Besides the aforementioned Hispanic (not Latin, she had corrected him on that) woman and the curly redhead next to him, there is one more female at the table and three dudes. He didn't much care about the dudes at this point, and since he had just struck out, without even trying, with the second of three, that left only the jock. Her name was Mackenzie, although most call her Mac.

Thinking to himself, maybe, just maybe, he could sort out an angle with her. Let's keep her in reserve since opportunities will arise during the next couple months. I'll trial and error with strangers and get her later. It might be hard to hold her off till then, but it will be good for him to be disciplined and feel this one out. There is something different about the jock, a confidence brought on by competition, a physical prowess from all the training and a nonchalant you-can't-hurt-me attitude, perhaps. He can tell she is a leader and is used to being in charge. He hopes she has his all-time favorite trait, the love of throwing a man down and taking him like there is no tomorrow. Nothing like being shown through action someone's lust for you. He would have to be careful with her though, in case the rumors about her are true.

Looking around the table, John figures it's a good idea to really check out the dudes "Not in that way, you perv," he thinks to himself, "but in a who's-gonna-have-my-back-and-save-my-ass-if-needed, kinda way." Not because he likes the dudes, but because that's just the code of a Tripper. "We go in together. We come out together." It's one of their mottos. It's in the creed. So far it seems to be in the genes of every Tripper he has met and all the stories he heard from Grandpa as a child. Grandpa did small unit type stuff in the Marines and he always focused on that part, the not-being-left-behind part, to a fault it almost seemed at the time. He inferred it in his stories frequently and often. They lived or died, together.

John looks at who is sitting at the head of the table. Grey was the name the man gave everybody at first introductions. Knowing what John knows about him now, it is almost too fitting to be his birth name. Between his mysterious past and his current physique, this guy is almost surreal. If he wasn't six feet tall you would think he was a dwarf of mystical lore. His mostly grey beard,

grown long, is salted with red and shades of brown. It is hard to tell how old he is. His face and hair show his age, a weathered fifty-ish, but his body and mind seem in tip top shape. He has the body of a thirty year old, and a mind sharply tuned by many a mission. John has to admit that this man has impressed him a lot already. Rosa calls the man Gunny and John, seeing how it complemented his grandpa's stories about Gunnery Sergeants, is going with it; "Always follow gunny and always do as you're told. He will get you home." Grandpa used to say. He was the guy to listen to. Do what he says when it hits the fan and it's mission change time; Grey has been through it many a time. He would have to be in charge of a Tripper crew. The minimum is twenty missions to even be eligible for the position of Lead on a crew. And it is an elected position, which is pretty amazing if you think about it. One: This is a military-like, government funded organization. Two: Trippers aren't allowed to vote for political offices or anything like that. With their ability (read permission) to go back in time, they could change too many things. Wouldn't it be amazing to be able to go back in time and make Mom president of the United World? Talk about power. Talk about getting laid, John thinks and snickers.

Sitting to Grey's right is probably John's ultimate goal, the soccer jock. She is fine as silk, his game will have to be just as smooth to land her.

Everybody has their quirks and hers is amazingly out of character for her type. She is a cigar smoker, a fine cigar smoker; apparently full strength 60-gauge cigars are her favorite. Enough said on that.

In between the jock and Rosa sits Charles. This guy is something else, definitely a well-trained hit man, even before this organization found him. He is also a nightly pot smoker, a hit-man pot smoker. Who knew they existed? This guy has the semblance of Charles Bronson. If he had the mustache, one would think he was. John thinks Bronson is probably in his lineage somewhere.

On the same side of the table as John, and to June's right sits an even bigger mystery than Grey. This guy is a freak, well, to John at least. He is quiet as can be. This guy's introvert tendencies are the complete opposite of John. John finds himself continually trying to get inside his shell, yet to no avail. Miokel (pronounced "Mi-oh-kel") is his name, and he is Grey's second in command. Having more missions under his belt than Grey, he would be in charge if he so desired. Instead he prefers not to be the face but "the business part of the team" as Grey had stated to him, June, and Mackenzie during their first meeting. John knows little of Miokel at this point, except he seems to be of Middle Eastern, desert-dweller descent based on his skin tone, Persian or Ottoman to go way back, although the pony tail hair length has John mystified. Based on what little he

knows of that culture, they are not known for pony tails. John is one to get answers when things intrigue him, and his curiosity level is pretty high on this guy.

Grey's voice finally breaks through John's thoughts. "Ok, ladies and gents, that is about all I have, and since there is not a question among you," Grey generally did not ask if there were questions or concerns, "we will adjourn and meet back here in 70 minutes. Enjoy your downtime."

The Tripper team suddenly awakens and fills the room with commotion as Mackenzie aka the jock, addresses Grey one on one. "Downtime before game time, huh?"

"Absolutely, rookie! We discovered there is nothing better than alone time before a mission to gather wits and center one's self. This is a different game than the one you are used to," winking, he smacks her on the shoulder playfully. "Speaking of different, that John character has a crush on you, just letting you know." Grey looks over his eyebrows at her.

"Bullshit", she rebuts. "He hasn't hit on me one time. He's hit on everyone but me several times, including Mildred, over at the lunch counter."

"Exactly," Grey states as he walks away.

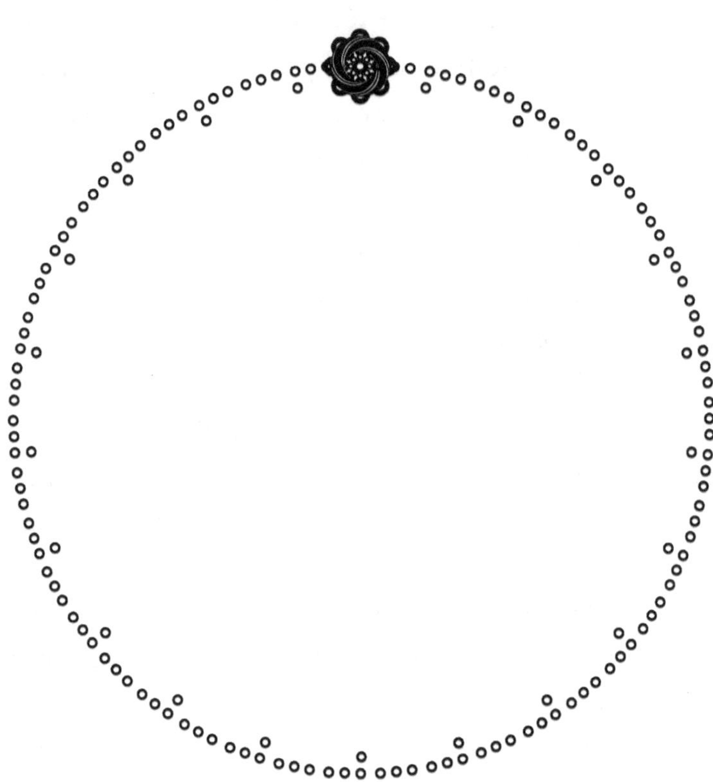

CHAPTER FIVE

Walking out the door Grey performs a mental check-off of final details. He needs to do it now, before his pre-game ritual.

Grey thinks to himself, "A nap. Yep. I take naps, and I am good with it," he smirks a little bit. Grey likes to take naps, power naps, cat naps, anything ten minutes or under. A long nap is what he calls sleep—two hours, four hours. Rarely does James Grey sleep more than six hours straight; only in extreme circumstances, like after a long mission or after taking on that crazy big burly Cajun. The pain killers they gave him made him sleep for a day or two. He was never quite sure how long he had slept.

Walking into an elevator, Grey finishes his mental checklist during the ride. Then, knowing he has covered it all, he dismisses the list from his mind. He has this part down pat, most of the parts in fact. It is impossible to

know everything and preplan every aspect of a mission, but this part is firm and handled.

Exiting the elevator, he moves down a hall that is mostly empty. What few people he comes across have their heads down just like he does; moving in their own little worlds, the bosses of this world focus on plans, and managing their people. No need for pleasantries around here.

Other benefits of the senior housing floors include: bigger apartments, a lesser population density, and bans on lower ranks entering the area—all translate to less traffic. Senior staff lives in the quietest section of the entire complex, a welcome respite for those in charge.

Reaching his door, Grey enters his unlocked apartment, no reason to lock doors here. Finding comfort in his modest bachelor decorations, he takes his boots off and heads straight for the fridge. Grabbing the juice, he spins off the cap and takes a long draw on it. Replacing the OJ, he grabs the cranberry juice and repeats the pattern. Reaching into another area of the fridge he grabs a vitamin bottle, opens it and pours two into his hand. After a thought, he adds another. Who knows when he will be back at his fridge? At least two days based on the basic plan, but it could be at least three times that, worst case.

After years of this, he has learned not to make personal plans for, well, for anything ever. Just going with the flow seems to work best for him while off mission; no

commitments, no tie downs. Still lots of sex, gratuitous at times. There are advantages to his job for sure. Even at his age, he had many to choose from, and fuck, at his age why the hell not. The older he gets the fewer inhibitions he has. Perhaps he is making up for lost time, or is it because he figures his odds are going to tip against him at some point?

He is the most senior Tripper as it is. Most didn't make it this far. Just the stress factor alone broke quite a few and death took just as many, sometimes strange deaths. Grey remembers his side mission partner getting drawn and quartered while on a trip, an image that will never be forgotten!

Watching a sight such as that will keep one focused on the fact that most people they come across on a mission will not believe that the Trippers have good intentions. Some couldn't care of their intentions anyway.

The aforementioned being a great example: the team he was a newbie member of accidentally landed their trip into some Sheik's harem. It didn't matter who they were, and it's not like it could be explained that they are time travelers. All the Sheik and his harem knew was that these weirdly dressed men all appeared from nowhere into the middle of the harem, causing chaos amongst the women. When questioned by the Sheik's torturers as to their intentions, James Grey's partner caved, almost instantly in fact, so quickly that the Sheik had him drawn and quartered for dishonoring himself with such a horrible made-up story. Time travel? Change the future? Such witchery!

The Sheik's version of drawn and quartered would be a sight as horrible as the first, every time it is seen—one limb hooked to a horse times four. Then on the given signal all riders ride in four different directions until—.

Years of practice allow the memories to go in and out of their tiny little memory boxes quickly and efficiently. Feelings are never allowed out of their boxes. The memories occasionally, but the feelings never.

After removing his boots, he lies back on his sleeper and closes his eyes. Amazingly, even with memories like these, Grey does indeed fall asleep.

He goes eyes open nine minutes later, ready to go, his cat nap a success. A few more pre-mission rituals and he will be good to go. Optimistic about this mission, he is excited to break-in the rookies. It's always a great idea to get that cherry popped as soon as possible; before tension and fear is built; fear is the death of the mind after all.

CHAPTER SIX

June looks in the mirror one last time, glad with her choice to not wear a hat and leave her curly locks free to bounce and glow. Heading for the door she pauses to look around her pad. She doesn't know when she will be back. Although she was told they will hold her apartment exactly as is for as long as she is employed there, she still takes a good long look, perhaps knowing that she will not be the same person the next time she walks into her place.

She opens the door and steps over the threshold into the hall. Instantly, she is engulfed by the noise and chaos of the hallway. It seems everyone at the complex is walking by her: techs, military personnel, a maintenance man, and even the lunch lady, Mildred, are hurrying to get where they are going. She is caught up in the rush, and starts hurrying her way towards the ready room.

The team is to meet there and go to the launch room all together. After a leisurely "last meal," as the Trippers call it, the crew will walk to the T.R.M. as a unit. June is seriously looking forward to what the senior team members called a "tram ride," even though she knows it will not fit the street car image held in her memory.

On her way there she allows herself to think about Loren. Wondering if he has found the note she left him on the fridge, she hopes he will be okay and will understand where she is coming from. There is no way she can maintain a relationship while learning her new job. Not this one. It will be strange enough as it is without learning how to be a partner with someone at the same time, something she has never quite figured out. Being a partner that is.

Since he is the lead tech for the mission she is about to embark on, her mission head just hopes Loren will still be focused in the moments they need him to be and is sure he will be. He was chosen for a reason. They all were.

The other parts of her don't want him to get hurt.

Rounding a final corner, she heads for the ready room door. Just before she gets within reaching distance, June is able to see through the door's windows. She spots most of the crew milling about and chatting. Some seem nervous. Others just seem like they are talking sports with nothing more than that on their minds. It's amazing how nervous June actually feels. This is her first mission and, the perfectionist that she is, June wants to do everything just right. No screw ups. And this is her chance to put her best foot forward. "No screw ups," she says under her breath.

Suddenly, John's hand appears on the door handle in front of her. "Did someone say screw?"

He pulls the door open, smiling at June wryly. "After you, my lady," he says charmingly. She stands there. "Please, if you would," he insists genuinely.

"Thanks, John. Much appreciated." June walks into the room.

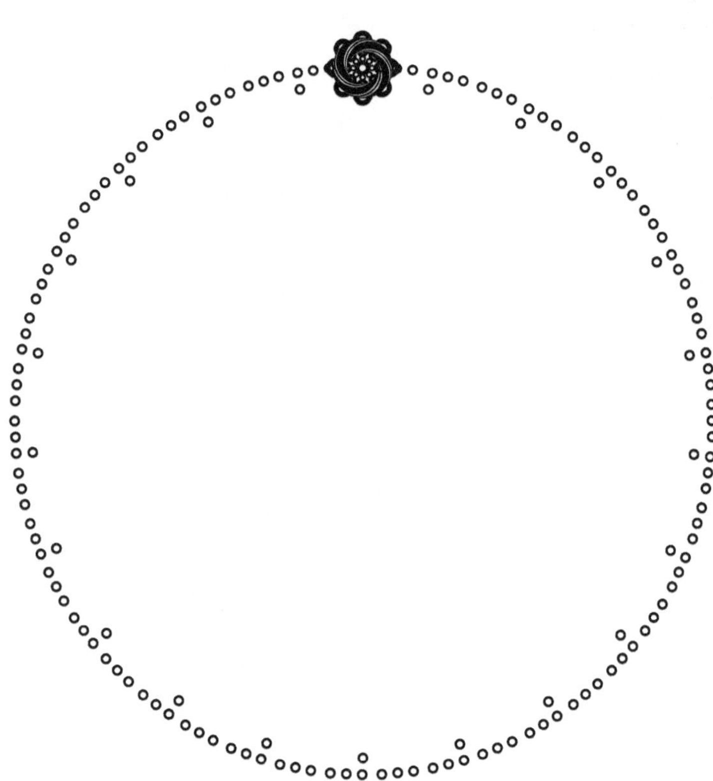

CHAPTER SEVEN

With the arrival of John and June, the gang is all here, and Grey starts the meeting. Well, meeting is really the wrong word for it. Pre-mission speech is more appropriate.

"All right, listen up. It's game time, except that cliché doesn't really apply 'cause this isn't a game, is it? I don't need to tell you guys the importance of this and every mission. We are the lucky mutha-fuckers that some crazy bastard in charge thinks should be going back in time and playing with the historic timeline."

Everybody laughs.

"They, in their infinite wisdom, think it's a good idea for John to go play with ancient computers and for June to use her, um, wits," he winks at her, "to influence history. Rosa gets to kick some ass on this mission AND lead a side mission for the first time. Rest assured this is not the first time she has kicked some ass, just her first lead." Grey looks at her with respect. "Congrats, Rosa, I can't wait to talk to you afterward." She laughs through her nose, trying to stay stone faced while inside she is running all possible scenarios through her head, knowing none of them will happen as thought or planned.

"All of us were literally handpicked by the best computers in the world for our specific traits and personalities to be matched together into a team," then firmly, "my team." He pauses.

"Don't let there be any question about that."

Grey looks each team member in the eye. He can tell there is no doubt that they will follow him; they will let him lead them. Good, he is insistent on that. There is no room for bullshit here. Grey had been on teams early on in which the leader didn't lead or some team member thought he knew better. In those cases, team members usually died.

"Good, glad we are on the same page."

Grey pauses again to think for a moment.

"That goes for my breakout team leaders also. They are the dictators on those teams for lack of a better word. There is no questioning their authority. Question all the local time frame authorities you want, just not each team leader." Chuckles all around on that one.

"Now, that is a speech you will never hear again from

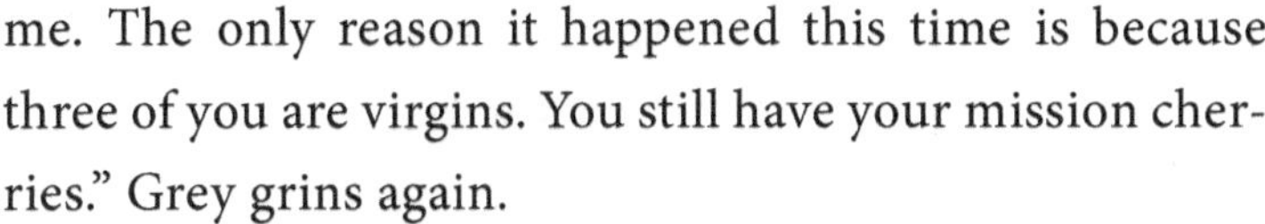

me. The only reason it happened this time is because three of you are virgins. You still have your mission cherries." Grey grins again.

No one else does.

"Don't worry, it will be fun. (He pauses between each of his next words for effect.) This—is—what—you—are—made—for. Enjoy the ride. It is possible to have fun and be a professional." Just a couple chuckles on that one.

Grey takes stock and looks around the room. He sees boredom in a couple and nervous anticipation in most. This seems about right to him.

"So, the strangest thing that ever happened to me on a mission is: when I was sent to take someone out and I realized it was my ancestor," Grey puts that out into the room.

Rosa chimes in next. "The strangest thing that ever happened to me on a mission is: while I was visiting my old period in time after two years of time travel, I realized nothing had changed because it was the same time frame as when I had left." She grins sheepishly.

Charles speaks up, a rarity for him. "Another glitch in the system sent me to kill myself. Apparently I fit the profile," he jokes, "or something like that," with seriousness in his voice.

"A scary thought," John says under his breath.

Charles continues, "Luckily, we all figured it out before I ran into myself."

Rosa pipes in, "Knowing you, you would have shot yourself due to your extreme dedication."

Charles grins, "True that!"

Grey glances at Miokel to see if he is going to play the game today. He is lost in thought. Grey moves on.

Addressing the new team members, Grey continues, "Life as you know it has changed and is about to change more than you can fathom. The story bits you just heard are true and can only be the experiences of someone like you." Looking at each of them: John, June, and Mackenzie, "Someone who travels through time for a living. . .has it sunk in yet? I know you were brought here from your respective times, yet for most, that is just the beginning of your surreal experience. Now is the time for the experience part. Stick to your buddies and do as you are instructed, and you will be fine. Remember, the first few moments upon arrival can be confusing as all get out. Just keep telling yourself it is real, and your mind will adjust faster."

Grey glances over to Miokel and asks, "Are we good?"

"We are good. You didn't miss a thing, which is par for the course," Miokel says grinning.

"Ok then, let's do it. Grab your gear. Let's go!"

CHAPTER EIGHT

The Colonel asks, "Is it true they all die?"

Mr. Roberts answers, "Yes, it is true, something to do with how traveling through the 'Einstein hole' causes all electrical energy to cease moving. You will have to ask a tech for a more detailed answer than that," Mr. Roberts states humbly, "even though we have devised a suit to revive them. The suit consists of a built-in bullet proof vest, a communicator, a mini defibrillator, and the list goes on, but it's basically the go-to vest, or war vest, for the Trippers. Sometimes the small charge provided by the suit is not enough to wake the heart from the travel trauma, so the Leaders usually have a more powerful AED on them, and the smart ones have another experienced crew member carry one as well."

Colonel Petzer leans back in his chair a bit, runs his hands through his chopped hair, and leans forward again, starting to grasp the obvious. The obvious being: his new assignment is career dream OR career disintegrator, depending on how the next couple years goes. What Mr. Roberts doesn't know is that Colonel Petzer has been sent here to bring this project to the next level. Extreme funding is on its way, and the Colonel is here to ensure it is spent in the best interest of the Powers That Be.

"Needless to say, the Trippers are true bad asses," the Colonel makes fact. "They are an elite group, and I do hope we are treating them as such. I am coming from running a Special Forces regiment and truly believe in making sure they know they are bad asses. Everyone else is in support of them. Support team, Bad Asses. Both are direly needed. Just . . ."

Mr. Roberts interrupts, "Some are bad asses, got it."

Knowing Mr. Roberts is humoring him, the Colonel decides to move on and ask for more details around the partly-told berserker story. "So, tell me about the Cajun," he requests.

"The Cajun?" Mr. Roberts asks, buying time while his mind switches gears. "Ah, the Cajun!" he exclaims. "The guy was a Brutus. He was recruited to fight. Um, how should I say this? Two giant body guards of the unbeatable kind. We were hoping he would whoop them into submission and then Grey could recruit them. Unfortunately, he couldn't handle the thought of dying,"

Mr. Roberts said wryly. "It wasn't the first time someone has kinda lost it. But it was the first time someone this dangerous actually went berserk en route to the launch area. We ended up killing him but not before he bashed up the place. He took out a couple techs and four members of the security team.

"On a side note, it's because of this incident that we relocated this control room way above the T.R.M., trip launch area. It's better anyway; we can look down into the launch room instead of having to watch it through the cameras."

Colonel Petzer asks, "But he didn't go after his team?"

"Not at all," Mr. Roberts says matter of factly, "which is the character loyalty we are looking for in Trippers. We need them to support each other at all costs. They are all they've got during a mission. He stayed loyal and protective of them to the end. And they, the team, stood by and watched the whole proceedings. In fact they kinda had to hold each other back from getting involved. Even though they were of sound mind and body, they still wanted to save him."

The Colonel says, "That's the kind of loyalty I looked for in my troops as well."

Andrew Roberts looks him in the eye, "Well, you can expect that trait in your Trippers."

Mr. Roberts can hear people milling around outside.

He knows it is the techs and other personnel waiting for them to finish so they can come in and do final prep.

"We had better find a different place to finish this conversation. They need to get the show on the road here and know better than to come in while we are talking."

Motioning for the door, "Would you like me to show you your new office, Colonel Petzer? We can finish the conversation there if you have time. I'm sure you'll want to be back here for the launch."

"Absolutely, wouldn't miss it for the world. Things always make more sense after seeing the reason for it all."

Mr. Roberts' eyebrows go in and down towards his nose, a sign he doesn't get what the Colonel is saying.

"Whenever I was tired of the BS that comes with dealing with politics, I would go down and watch the crafts where the troopers come and go. It would remind me that the battle I was fighting was so they can fight theirs with the right equipment and support. It is easy to lose track of that in all the minutia and bullshit. Is it not?"

Picking up his briefcase and heading towards the doors, Mr. Roberts can't help but nod in agreement. It is exactly the reason he is ready to move on from this gig and back to the world above ground. His love of the spies' world of intrigue, backstabbing, and betrayal, all in the name of the cause, feeds a part of him that only others like him could understand. These people down here are way too black and white for his tastes. He hopes they will never find out what all this is really about. He'll have to be sure to keep Colonel Petzer in the dark as well. The Colonel seems like he will fit in nicely down here. This place seems to need a military mindset of sorts, some black and white to rule the big gray areas of their missions.

Mr. Roberts is in agreement with the PAB's replacement choice. The Colonel's only downfall so far: he seems way too patriotic and loyal to his men to throw any of them under the bus if need be, a weakness in this spy's mind.

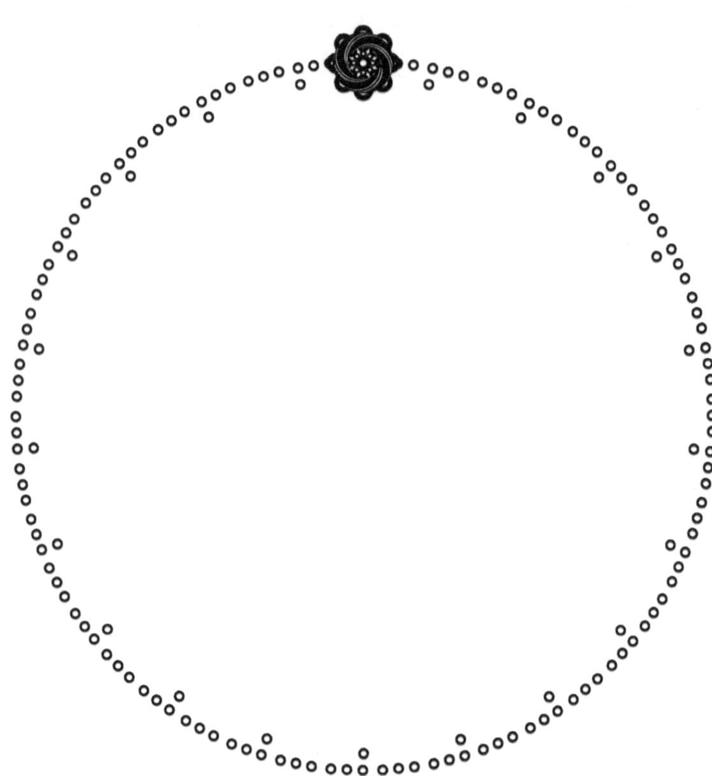

CHAPTER NINE

The crew stands up, gathers their things and heads out of the ready room in silence. This is something Grey asks for and more honestly, requires; feeling this helps set the tone and focuses his crew. He requires this for every mission launch: 'trip walk' as it is known to them.

James Grey is the type of leader who asks his team to do things for him, and they do, not because it's their job or chain of command. They do it because they want to. He is the kind of leader you want to please, want to do the right thing for. The worst thing ever would be letting him down. After all, he would die before letting you down.

This is of those reasons Rosa has a tendency to call Grey 'Gunny.' He reminds her of her gunnery sergeants back in the corps. It was their job to make sure all get home. They have a tendency to take it personally when one of their own is lost, almost like they were losing one of their own kids. When in all reality, it really is like that, maybe even worse.

Seven figures strut their way down the hall in total silence, total focus on their faces, all knowing full well the gravity of their situation. Grey's double check that they had not one, but two pocket AEDs removed all doubt of what could happen to at least one person on each launch. All Trippers will have to be resuscitated at least once in their inaugural year. It's a hard thing to accept indeed.

All team members wear the same base uniform for the launch. Each is adorned in a high tech jumpsuit, enduringly called the "tripper suit." Made out of an almost bombproof fabric, it is nearly indestructible. Having basic morphing abilities, it is a prime tool for the job. Nothing is better than an item of clothing that manages to switch to time- and location-appropriate styles while you are still trying to figure out if you tripped to the right place or not. The shoes are included in the same high tech arena as the suit. They too can morph initially and only by direct command later. Basically, they have a computer brain that chooses a look, usually morphing during the end of the travel period. The Trippers simply arrive in their new zone with the appropriate looks for that time period and mission, "simply" being the key word here. Upon close inspection, the locals, as we'll call them, would notice the missing details.

The more senior members have tailored their tripper suit to their needs over time, more or less pockets and places to hang things to keep handy. Grey, at one point, had to directly tell Rosa to stop adding places to hang explosives within her jumpsuit; although, he entirely agrees with her adage that you cannot have too many devices that explode. He still must put a limit; otherwise, when the inevitable of being shot at occurs, there will only be one direct result for her and those within a three-block radius.

The newbies generally just carry what they had been taught to carry in tripper school. By the end of their first trip there will be additional items in their pockets, and those items generally stay there until used. That is generically true for all Trippers, except for the Twinkie that Charles accidentally left in his suit during a trip back to 2114 from 1984. Apparently even a Twinkie can't stay fresh for 100-plus years of time travel. He figured since it wasn't really a food, the "food rule didn't apply." Boy was he wrong. When he awoke back at his home time it had grown into an entire and new type of ecosystem in his pocket. The lab rats quickly whisked it away, never to be seen again . . . he hoped.

The back of the tripper suit is adorned with their

controversial emblem. The saying "We go out together, we come back together" surrounds a picture of a Salvador Dalí-esque clock with legs, arms, and Einstein hair that is tripping on a worm hole and falling into it. The saying "Been then, it's different now" adorns the bottom in Latin.

And we say controversial . . . not enough people know about the program's existence to actually create a stir, but still, it's a bone of contention for some. They being of the mind that this is something to be taken seriously whilst the Trippers think they need to lighten up and maybe take a trip or two to change their perspective on life.

Grey walks slightly ahead of the next crew member, not because of superiority but because of his stride. This next crew member is a mere five feet ten inches. The quietest and most senior of the crew is also Grey's right hand man. Miokel has been on more missions than Grey even. Introverted, quiet, and all business, he is the first to think outside the box, and usually his first instinctual solution ends up being the best solution. In periods of time-sensitive decision making it is usually his ideas with which Grey goes.

The other five team members follow close behind, none of them speaking or grab-assing—a sure sign that they were ready and focused, and a good sign from a newly-formed team. Although some have trips under their belts, and this team has spent the last few months training together, this is still their first mission as a team. Grey is confident in his team. Not all of his team are as confident in themselves; this will have to change, soon.

Reaching the swinging doors adorned in their emblem, Grey and Miokel open them. The need for security personnel or locks is minimal here, the security system being a sinister combination of new technology and some of the oldest. About 20 feet before reaching the swinging doors, the building's computer system body-scans the approaching beings. Once it is done determining who they are, it makes a decision. If they are supposed to be there, nothing happens. If they are an animal or an unauthorized human, their section of the floor simply drops out, plunging the individual or unsuspecting cat into the pit below and closing the second the being falls through, trapping them below. Pitfalls are one of oldest and effective traps on the planet. Even in this modern age, gravity wins every time.

It is a short, straight walk from the swinging door entrance to the ramp heading up into the machine.

June catches her breath as she walks the ramps. The feeling of the machine was overwhelming. While it is still ramping up and not at full power (and won't be until the Trip is a go) the feeling of the hum in her body is making it hard to breathe. It fills her ears with pressure

more than sound, airwaves pushing against her chest causes everything cognizant to slow down; the sound is getting louder in her ears, her breathing tougher. Her knees start to wobble, and her eyes are going blurry, and in the nick of time she runs into the back of John. Hard. Full on. Groin to butt contact and everything. Suddenly the overwhelming effects of her body's adrenaline and endorphins goes away.

June mumbles, "I'll have to remember that bumping uglies with John has a sobering effect." Hearing this, he starts to turn around with one of his choicest pickup lines already prepared in his mind and sees Grey looking over his right shoulder back at him, daring him.

John turns back around just as they are about to enter the machine. Looking up for a bit before entering, he sees what seems like ten stories of machine over him and a substantial amount to either side of the doorway as well. He wonders how much each of these trips costs the corp of corporations anyway. A billion dollars, maybe two; two was the biggest number John could think of that was reasonable, and he is sure that is still a substantial number even in this day and age. "The Machine," as it is affectionately known by all but a few, is a massive, intim-idating structure approximately 200 feet tall and who knows how long; there is only one end of the machine that's exposed.

The exposed end has a door at the end that only certain techs and the Tripper teams are permitted to enter. No other has entered and been allowed to live. Several curious members of the cleaning crew, a few unfortunate VIP guests, and one or two off-duty personnel entered the swinging doors below, never to be heard from again. Urban legend states they were shoved back in time never to be retrieved, placed in a time when they would come across as crazy or a lunatic if they tell their story. In all reality, they were probably killed by the PABs for trespassing into an area that doesn't exist on paper or at all to those outside the project.

All team members seem to slow as they approach the machine. None can resist the urge to look up at the vastness of it. Even Grey seems to glance up and sneak a peek at it. Those in the team who haven't experienced it before are obviously overwhelmed at the vastness, and are gaining an overwhelming feeling of being a little black ant in a giant's world.

As he approaches, John can hear a hum in his ears coming from the machine. He can feel the hum of the machine throughout his entire body. Every particle in his cells is vibrating from the ambiance of the air around him. The ground is vibrating; it feels as if he is standing on a giant orbital sander. He has a quick and painful brain image of every bolt shaking out of its proper place in the

giant machine, not all at once, but one at a time so no one would notice until it, in its entirety, fell onto the team.

"Nah," he finds himself verbalizing, removing the thought from his fear place.

Luckily everyone else is so in their own moment that they don't hear him talking to himself.

Walking through the entry door, they enter a hall-way-like section dimly lit by LED lights in the walls, then through a section of black lights, and then next through what feels like an electric field of the sort designed to kill off any and all parasites, bugs, fungi, and any other unwelcome living things. Once through the "life kill-ing" section, the machine opens up into a small ware-house-like room. As one enters the huge room, a giant window section can be seen up and off to the left. A wide platform seems to hover at the top of a long flight of metal stairs. The static in the air increases as the team climbs the flight of stairs. The hairs on the body slowly rise to attention. Every hair: leg, pubic, and head hair tries to remove itself from the body.

Everything is abuzz with electricity.

The crew turns to the right and each approaches their designated position. There are seven four-foot cir-cles marked on the concrete, one per Tripper. Standing with their backs to the window above them, each crew member does a last-second gear check, ensuring all their

wanted and required items are with them and contained within the four-foot diameter. It always sucks to have an item not make the journey because it wasn't self-contained within the circle.

Looking down from the window, the Colonel feels excited to see his first launch. It is amazing luck that there is one on his first day. He feels like a kid getting ready to watch a show, he suddenly smells popcorn and wishes for a giant bag to nervously devour. He watches the team walk up onto the platform. Then, strange to him, they all turn away from the window and take their positions in marked circles, spreading out in a bowling pin-like layout. The team leader stands at the point and the rest of the team is distributed behind him, first, second, third in increasing numbers with the last man standing alone in the center at the rear of the formation.

From behind Colonel Petzer, Loren says, "We are ready sir."

"Then let's do it. You have permission to launch."

Loren, talking to intercom of sorts, "We are a go up here, sir."

Down below, Grey looks around at his people. Glancing left and right over each of his shoulders, Rosa is over his left shoulder, Miokel over his right, Mackenzie, June, and John, the newest members of the crew, are next. Behind them Charles is standing with his hand over his left chest pocket. If he didn't know him better, Grey would think he was pledging allegiance to the flag. Charles glances up from his pocket and nods to Grey.

Grey, speaking to the voice in his ear says, "Trippers ready."

To his crew Grey yells, "Game on, people. Enjoy the ride!"

Loren pauses, listening to a voice in his ear. He reaches down and quickly types commands into the keyboard and pushes enter with a little, happy flair.

Colonel Petzer watches intently. Quickly his smile gets bigger than it's been since he was a kid. Down below the energy is intense. It can be "felt" through the viewing window. As the energy rises, the wall in front of the team below becomes less solid. It seems to become fluid and yet still stand tall as a wall should. Suddenly it starts to morph. Its overall form and shape still flat and wall-like, twists from the center as if a pencil was stuck in it and spun to the right. The edges of the wall hold tight to its form while the masses between the edges and the center torque and twist from the battle of energy and opposing forces. Suddenly, the center appears to expand towards the team reaching towards Grey at the point. Reaching and reaching, the center suddenly revolts from its desire to grab Grey in its embrace and lunges itself quickly away from him, pulling the rest of the wall mass in with it. The Colonel's attention, so engrossed with the wall, doesn't notice a force-field of sorts developing around each team member.

The air outside of each of the tripper's position is in turmoil; the air inside each of their cylinders is perfectly still. The obligatory pieces of dust and paper are flying about the place while each team member stands like stone inside their cylinder of protection. Seeing their backsides, the Colonel can only wonder at the expressions on their faces. Without warning, the seven cylindrical pods zip towards the now liquid wall and are enveloped by it.

As soon as Charles, the last man, is engulfed by the energy, Loren hits a few more keys.

The room below goes still.

The dust and paper flying around suddenly clings to the walls from all the static. It holds there as the energies subside, finally finding their lazy way to proper resting places on the floor.

Above, Colonel Petzer is smiling big and for a great reason. He just watched seven people vanish into thin air.

Loving his new gig, he walks away, hands clasped behind his back, smiling and thinking what it would be like to disappear and reappear in another time frame. Maybe some day he will find out. For now, he walks out and heads to his new office. Time to see if his predecessor has left any celebratory liquor stashed in a desk or cabinet drawer.

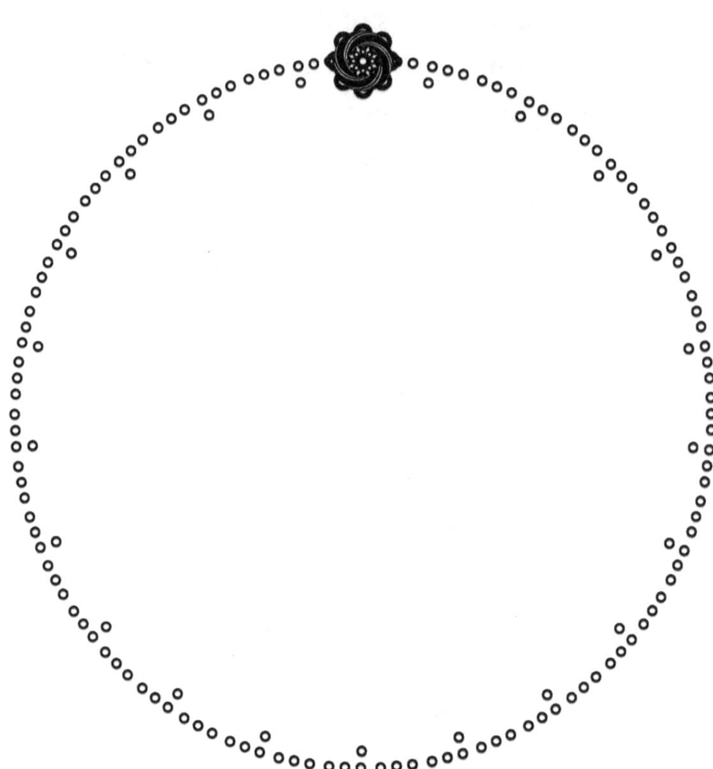

CHAPTER TEN

John is swimming in a vast sea of gel, somehow almost being able to breathe it, he struggles for breath and tells himself to breathe. BREATHE. Breathe. BREATHE, dammit!

Suddenly, his body lifts a few feet in the sea.

"I think I was just zapped by an eel! What the fuck?" His body tingles from center to extremes. Suddenly the gel goes thin, and thinner still.

He pops his eyes open to see Charles kneeling over him smiling a big mischievous grin. Charles' AED in hand he asks John, "Want another for good measure?"

Realizing his heart had stopped; John's heart skips a few beats and speeds up. A frantic feeling overcomes him.

Charles says, "Now relax there, tough guy! It's all good now. You've gotten your first death out of the way. Life is easier from now on." Charles grins even bigger.

Looking around, John sees the rest of the newbies scanning their surroundings in ever-increasing acceptance that the bill of goods they had been sold was for real. They have indeed traveled from one time to another.

Looking down at himself, John realizes he had died. His heart had failed to restart with the auto-defibrillator built into his suit. He hopes this was a fluke and is not going to be an occurrence every time. Feeling around on his suit, checking it to make sure it contains a defibrillator, being of the sort, he has checked before. Still, he follows the wires through his suit, feeling both the two end shockers and something like a battery pack. It does indeed contain one. He'll have to remember to mention it to the techs on their return. Fuck! Better yet, find time on the mission to make sure everything is in good working order *before* the trip back to 2114.

The team is in what appears to be an old wooden outbuilding. The inside consists of plain untreated wood; various hooks exist in a haphazard pattern on the walls. Some hold old rakes, hoes, and pruners. Some hold nothing at all. Miscellaneous belts, and old, often-sharpened chainsaw blades adorn others. Dust and dirt and more of both, lay over everything and everywhere. Years of wood shavings, dirt, and filings lay about a workbench area. The floor may have been concreted slate stone, but appears as dirt and stone in its current state.

An animal has clawed and chewed a 1/3 meter hole in one area of the structure. There are recent signs of passage in both directions. The tracks lead to a pile of seven straw bales piled in a corner where another like-size hole creates an entrance to a warm, dry den inside.

Junk and various farm-type collectibles lay about the place. Each of the four corners hold various pieces of wood, metal, and barrels, all unceremoniously placed in a general direction, none having been touched or moved in ages.

Grey eyeballs his team, especially his new three. Mac and June seemed to be working on acceptance. They are indeed in a different place than they were a few minutes ago, a strange thing to accept for all. John is tracing the pathways of his suit's AED, his way of dealing with the fact that on his very first trip, he awoke to the rude sight of Charles' ugly mug, fanatical smile, and the sobering fact that he just had his ass shocked back to life. Waking to a Charles close-up with his 1,000-yard stare can be a rude enough awakening as it is. Add in the paddles and whoa!

And John is handling it like a champ.

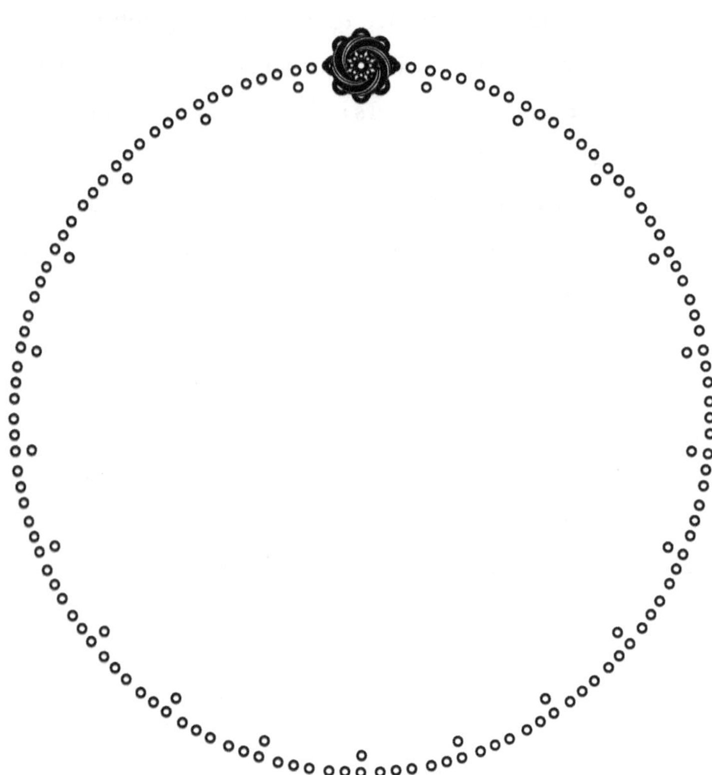

CHAPTER ELEVEN

Rosa, a pro at these trips, is alert as soon as she is conscious in their new time. Scanning the situation, she sees it all in order; Charles already on the dead John situation, and all others either moving or breathing. Gathering her wits, she strengthens her arms and pushes herself into a sitting position, then gathering her heels to her butt she wills strength to her legs and stands up. Her immediate mission is on her mind.

It is her job to secure the outside area of the building. Having been told to expect no immediate threats, she unclips her pistol cover and lifts the 1911 into its accustomed position in her hand. Happy to be in a time frame where she can still carry her favorite side arm, Rosa readies herself. Military intelligence can be an oxymoron after all.

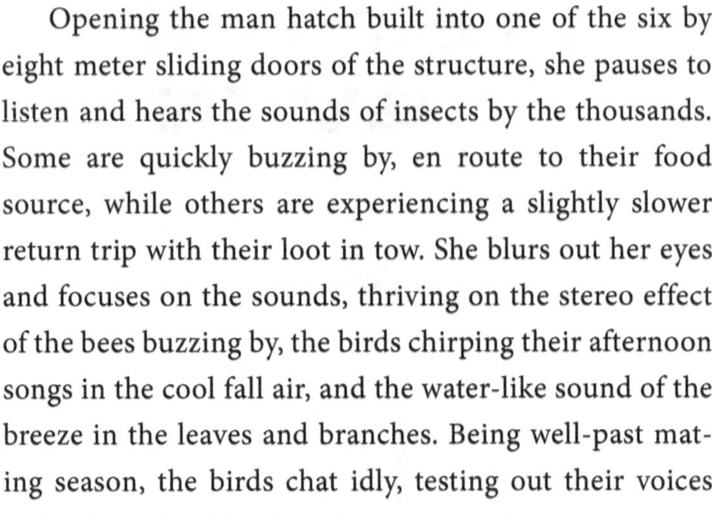

Opening the man hatch built into one of the six by eight meter sliding doors of the structure, she pauses to listen and hears the sounds of insects by the thousands. Some are quickly buzzing by, en route to their food source, while others are experiencing a slightly slower return trip with their loot in tow. She blurs out her eyes and focuses on the sounds, thriving on the stereo effect of the bees buzzing by, the birds chirping their afternoon songs in the cool fall air, and the water-like sound of the breeze in the leaves and branches. Being well-past mating season, the birds chat idly, testing out their voices and calling for friends before starting their journeys to warmer climes. Having no intentions of being caught this far north when the weather changes, their instincts are willing them to travel any day now.

That same breeze moves grasses and is rattling a few leaves, none of the dead ones yet matted on the moist ground, just multitudes on the limbs.

Sniffing the air, she smells dampness, rotting apples, fresh country air, some stale barn air, but not much else. She notices no telltale signs of human danger, no smells of sweat, running engines, or food.

Reassured, Rosa steps through the mantle. She pauses, listens and steps the following leg through. Closing the door as she commits to the outdoors, she flattens herself to the wall. To the left and right nothing can be

seen but old orchards. Abandoned some time ago, all are being restored to nature's way of growing. None of the trees have the highly pruned look of an active orchard. Crouching down and resting on her haunches as she had been taught long ago, she listens some more. Hearing the same as before; she starts visually scanning the area, not in a moving sweep but in a grid-like pattern. She places her eyes in an area for a bit, then moves them slightly. She un-focuses them again in a different area. Looking for movement and odd shapes is best done from unfocused, unmoving eyes. Rosa knows from experience that if she is looking for one thing in particular, she will be more likely to miss something else. So, keeping preconceived thoughts from the mind while looking for anything will help her instincts to do their thing.

Once more she closes her eyes and focuses on the smells. Taking deep breaths, slowly she tastes the air. Same as before, just no stale barn air.

Her instincts agree with her other senses' idea of no threats; she regains her feet for the second time in minutes. Walking counter clockwise around the structure, she continues to scan visually and aurally.

Giving everything the all clear, she relaxes for a moment; grateful for the remote location and John's awesome, professional response to being non-responsive. She eases her mind a bit. Returning her pistol to

its holster hidden in the outer layers of her suit, Rosa continues to walk in an ever-increasing distance around the building. Glancing back at the structure, in need of paint but of sound roof, she takes in their home for the next few days, stopping one more time for a listen before making a beeline back inside the outbuilding and relaxing a bit more.

Walking back to the main door, she gets her bearings using the afternoon sun and surmises where their target location is: another farm just a few miles away. Painting a picture in her head, she enters home base. Almost. She pauses and then turns and crouches with her back to the open door. Being a product of war, chaos, and other not-so-great parts of human existence, she realizes the surreality of the environment she is in. Getting a little teary-eyed, she takes the time to close her eyes. Turning towards the sun, she revels in the heat it creates on her face, how she can see through the membranes of her eyelids. With her face still turned towards the sun, she turns her focus onto the buzzzzz of the insects. Quiet enough to hear the bugs flying by is new and a little alien to her. Zzzooomnnnm, maybe it's just a bee flying by. A lower droning noise heads her way. Now alarmed, she opens her eyes in time to see a heavily-ladened bumble bee drone by. Its legs full of yellow pollen, they hang, unable to be tucked up against the body, they cause a bumbling

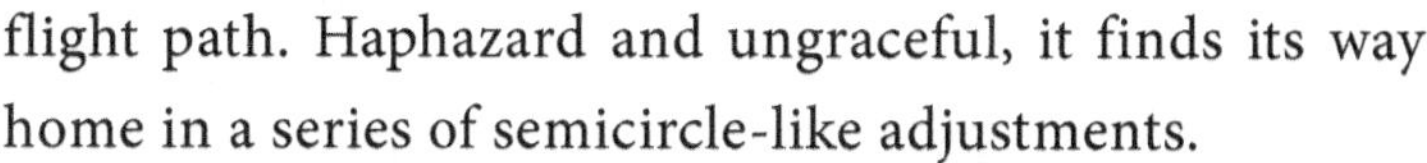

flight path. Haphazard and ungraceful, it finds its way home in a series of semicircle-like adjustments.

Closing her eyes for just a second more causes a smile to escape from her face. It cracks open the instant it is allowed, showing her joy in the moment.

Turning, eyes still closed, she steps through the door.

Opening her eyes, pausing for a second as they adjust, she notices the musty, rusty smell of the barn again. She sees the rest of the crew gathering around Grey as he builds a model of their target, wasting no time as usual.

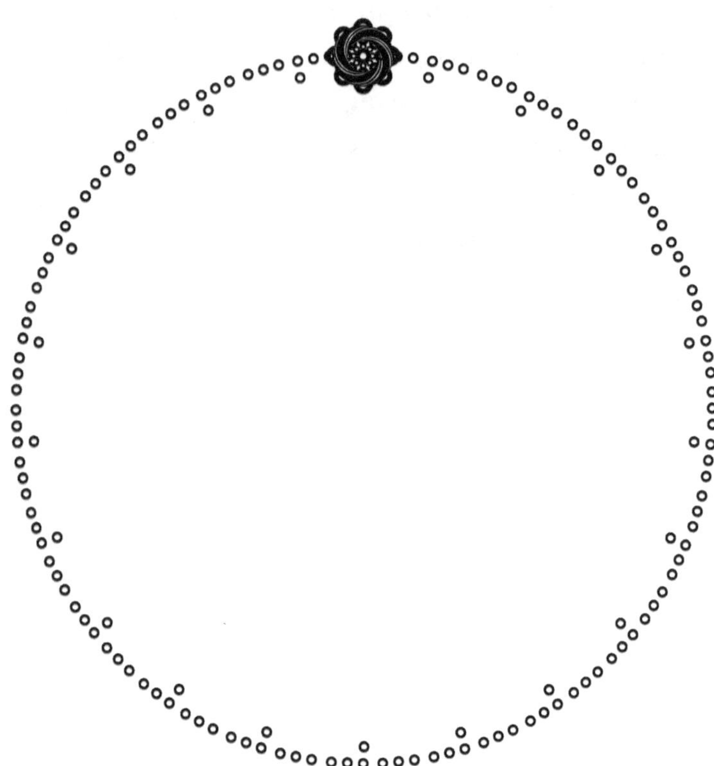

CHAPTER TWELVE

Nobody says anything. They all watch as Grey builds a replica from his mind. Only he and Miokel have the target details in their brains. All others are on a need to know basis; they have been in the dark as to what they are in for.

Grey finishes his homemade mockup of their intended target, leans up after having been hunched over focusing on the details of his layout, and checks one more time before he calls out to his crew.

"Ok, let's gather 'round." He looks up and sees they are already gathered and ready. Grey smiles and says, "Great response time. I'll accept no less from now on."

A few chuckles escape from the group.

"Before we go any further, congrats to John for popping his cherry. Since he was the first of the rookies to die of a lazy heart, he gets the award!"

"Awesome, what is it?" Johns asks.

"TBD, John, TBD," Grey responds.

Laughs all around.

Charles nudges John playfully.

In his best announcer voice, Grey says, "Now for the moment you've all been waiting for . . . why we are here?" Pointing at the mock-up, he says, "Here is a replica of another abandoned farm about three clicks from here as the crow flies. Luckily, there is a small mountain between us and them so we don't have to worry about sound discipline too much."

Realizing he forgot that part in his mock-up, he reaches down and mounds up a couple piles of dirt along one side of the farmstead and draws an arrow in the dirt to represent the direction they are going to be coming in from. Then, as a second thought, adds another range on the other side of the farmstead as well.

"Basically, we are surrounded by old mountains in an area of a country that is more or less abandoned. We will set up Observation Posts as overwatch and to gather intelligence as to patterns of any possible guards and sentries just in case it's needed. One of those two teams will stay as overwatch and come down after everybody else's departure for cleanup. The other will enter the compound shortly after my team's arrival and assist. The location is being used as a secret research facility. We are to obtain all pertinent data and at least one scientist, if possible."

Mackenzie exclaims, "Wait! We have to kidnap people?"

Looking at her he replies, "If possible." He continues, "We will take the information," looking at John, "probably contained on a few computers. We can take the hard drives instead of taking the entire computer." Grey grins.

"If possible," John says, grinning back.

June asks, "What is the big deal? What are they doing? Why do we want it?"

Miokel speaks up, "Great questions, June. We may find that out as we go, but right now, we are in the dark on that one." He looks at Grey, knowing there is a great chance he already knows but hasn't said. Miokel learned a long time ago that Grey knows way more than he shares; the who's and why's are irrelevant to him. Accomplishing the mission is what matters most to Grey, and Rosa too, for that matter.

"Rosa, Mac, Charles, and Miokel will head out soon and set up OPs. John, you and June are with me. We will be heading in the front gate of the farmstead."

"Any questions? No? Good. Miokel I want you guys to head out in about an hour or less, grab some chow, and then hit it."

"The J's," staring right at June and John till they get the new nickname, "Grab some chow, and we'll cover some more details in a bit."

Pausing, he knows he forgot something. "Oh, yeah, no comms on this one!"

Rosa lets out an, "Old school, love it." Addressing the rookies, "For some reason the technology we bring with us doesn't always work."

"Or at other times the locals, as I call them, have the technology to spot our technology or listen in on our communications. Since we aren't really here we can't risk recordings of our existence." Miokel helpfully adds.

Moving off to a corner, John and June settle in for a little meal time while Grey has one last conversation with his right hand man, Miokel.

June sits down cross-legged on the loose straw and hay, while John chooses a pail to perch on.

"How are you feeling, John?"

"Um, not bad actually."

"What was it like?"

"If you mean dying, it was painless. I just wasn't cognizant of what was going on until an electric jolt went through my system and my eyes opened. I have no idea of what the trip was like though, no memories of it." Then he asks, "How about you June, what was the trip like?"

"I don't remember much of it either. It was dreamlike and almost like I wasn't in my body. I don't have a solid memory of the journey, just that I could feel something changing. It was like I could feel my body changing, not

like getting sick or growing old, it just felt different. This time we are in feels different also. I can't put a finger on it, but I can definitely tell we are not in "our" time frame. I was just getting used to the era we were in, how it felt, how electric it was, or should I say, how electric the area we now live in feels."

"I know what you are saying. I can feel it too, and I am from a time when it's all about electricity. Heck, even the colors were electric in my time!" John says with a wry grin.

"When are you from?" June asks laughing, "I am going to have to get used to asking that question, aren't I!"

"I am from 2054, a time of unabated information and chaos. Technology was advanced to the point that nothing needed battery replacement or a separate electric source. Even the smallest village in a third world country was able to get a hold of portable technological devices. Missionaries no longer carried books to teach their religions; they hand out computer pads like they are Gideon bibles. Technology is cheap and everywhere. I even saw reports of tech pads being dropped onto the villages deep in the mountains and jungles of Africa and South America. No one was in the dark anymore. I would wake up and grab my pad. While making a morning espresso, I would watch morning rituals from the deepest, darkest villages from within the tallest sky scraper in Tokyo, the tulip fields of Western Europe, and they would watch mine."

"Wait you mean everybody could watch anybody at will?"

"No, I had to approve it and so did they. Kinda like the Facebook profiles of the early 2010s, except it was live video feed mostly, not still pictures."

"Facebook?" true bewilderment from June.

"Facebook was a social site."

"Um, remember, I am from the pre-computer age. Computers in my day were in MIT and military warehouses. I do remember a—,"she blushes slightly, "—one friend of mine who was in the military intelligence field. He once took me to a computer. He wanted to do things on it and I was afraid it would electrocute me. It was the size of a warehouse!"

"Haha, I forgot when you are from!" John exclaims, "Facebook was a social site that all the sudden decided to focus on commercial marketing instead of connecting people socially and lost all of its following. In fact there were sites before them, and every ten years or so, a new one takes over when the current champ loses its way into the realm of greed."

June, still perplexed, says "I still don't know what you mean honey. I mean, in my time, being social was all about going out on the town, listening to music, and working hard to find a husband. With what little I know about you, John, I already know you would like it. You would love the fact that there were tons of women who believed their goal was to find a man. Women were either being trained to find and land a good husband or totally rebelling against the idea, like I was."

June laughs at the thought of John in her time frame. He would love being pursued as apposed to being the one rejected all the time. Even his shoddy game and pick up lines would have worked; some of the women around her age of thirty were down right desperate to find a man. Since all the men had returned from WWII, and taken many of the jobs back, finding a husband was a form of survival for many women.

June, not one to conform or stay home, found a way to survive and thrive in the booming city of 1950s Detroit. Instead of becoming a house wife, she found her way into grifting. Grifting was a way to use her wiles, wares and charisma to get her needs met; within a short period of time, she and a few others like her had a thriving business.

Before they could continue their conversation, Grey comes over to where they are sitting, "Ok, you two; you ready?"

John and June both sigh, brought back to their present situation by his voice.

"Or perhaps that story, first," June suggests, wanting to keep the current mood a little longer.

John shouts, "The big, bad, burly, Cajun story! Heck yah, I've been waiting for that one. It's infamous in training circles—what not to do on your first day!"

Grey replies, "Ok, OK, FINE! I'll tell the fuckin' story. Geesh. Why are humans enthralled by car accidents?" rhetorically asked.

Mackenzie, from across the room yells, "Cause they are fucked in the head! Seeing someone else's misery relieves us of ours."

John agrees, "Hard to argue with that logic!"

Those who were interested in the story gather around, either standing or sitting on the dirt encrusted floor. Before you know it, the entire team is gathered to listen; not much else to be doing right now, anyway.

It becomes apparent very quickly that Grey is a great story teller; it is just as obvious that the story he tells is not even close to the one Mr. Roberts fed Colonel Petzer.

CHAPTER THIRTEEN

Grey, breathing deep, goes into his mind and decides how to tell his new team, his current team, the only team that matters, how he didn't see one of his people losing it, going bonkers under his watchful eye, and Grey just figured it was the big guy's personality. It feels like a failure to Grey, not something he wants to be reminded about every time someone wants to hear about the infamous event.

June looks over at Grey, seeing some discomfort and assuming it was about story telling. "Just tell us like you were in a bar telling a story. Make it fun and intriguing."

"It was a dark and stormy night," Grey looks and smiles.

Then for real he starts his story; after another deep breath he says, "We recruited this guy to take on two badass body guards of some dude we needed to fall out of favor with his fellow business owners. He was the firm's

accountant and the favorite nephew of the mob boss known as Bruno. I know, strange name for a mob boss."

"What's his real name, Mr. Grey?" John's way of showing respect. Sir was never meant as a compliment when leaving his mouth.

Grey shrugs, "You know me and names," smiling, "These two body guards were the reason this lowly accountant was able to bully his way into the position of power behind the power. That, combined with Bruno's backing, gave the guy the wit to cajole the firm into laundering his uncle's funds, something strange for even a law firm, I am sure."

Grey pauses for effect.

"The two body guards were in it purely for the money, they had a five-year retirement plan. Nobody but them knew it, which was a smart thing in their line of work."

John nods, "We've all seen the movies. Retirement plans lead to death." He puts his finger in the air and says "Just one more job!" he does a good job of mocking just about every criminal depicted in the movies.

Grey continues, "They figured helping this pudgy accountant with the tough uncle was the quickest way to achieve their plan of traveling the warm parts of the earth until they found their perfect island to grow old and fat on! They negotiated a percentage of the take for protection pay, instead of the usual room and board plus

expenses bullshit. Escalating the nephew to the reins of the company was a sure way to increase their percentage, even if it probably meant the nephew was either going to jail or going to do something stupid with his new shit-ton of power and money, causing his uncle to be forced to cut him up as an example of who not to be, EVEN if you are the nephew of a mob boss named Bruno."

Rosa interrupts, "How is that important to the telling of why he went bonkers?"

"He's setting the tone," Mackenzie defends Grey's story telling.

Rosa laughs, "I don't care about the background. What does that have to do with how we all kicked his ass?"

"Leave him be. Let him tell his story." Charles, standing with his arms folded and leaning against the wall in his usual laid back version of the 'ready for anything position,' is smiling and enjoying Grey's story time.

Continuing, Grey adds, "We found this guy in the New Orleans outskirts living simply, and fighting for fun and money. He was known for a berserker mode he would go into if he was suddenly afraid he wasn't going to win. Instead of succumbing to that fear, his body, or mind, who knows, would put him in a berserker mode that would just demolish his opponent and sometimes the facility they were fighting in. Even a few innocent bystanders from time to time got caught up in the chaos and left the emergency room with stories to tell. His fights were always well-attended 'cause they were all hoping he would go berserk, even if it did mean they had a chance of being hurt!"

"Kinda like the old bull runs," Rosa says, thinking of her heritage.

"Or rubberneckers at accidents," June says, keying in on what Grey had said earlier, "something like that."

"Right! Regardless, he did great through the entire training. Was a smart dude with military experience, Army S.F., I think. Fun to hang with and all-around nice guy, to be honest. He just had this part of him that liked to fight, an angry side of him. Never did hear where it came from or if he always had it. He isolated himself more often than not, just like he did in New Orleans. We also had him on calming drugs for most of his training period, just in case; we had to wean him off it in order for him to be mission ready. Heck, I didn't even see any signs of it coming, his losing it, I mean. But that day, on the way into the TRM, he just lost it." Grey fades off into his own world for a moment.

Charles clears his throat to let Grey know he had left the building, lost in his head.

"As we approached the TRM that day, I remember suddenly feeling as if Miokel and I were walking alone. We stopped and turned around, and he was just stand-

ing there with his arms out holding everybody back. We immediately started back towards the crazy Cajun to see what the fuck was up. All the while, he was looking up at the large, loud, electrically charged machine, walking backwards slowly, pushing everyone else along with him. One of the team tries putting their hand on his back to stop his backward motion, and that sets him off! Spinning around, he runs them over.

"By the time the team got into the control room, he was already setting about wrecking the place. Techs and other things were flying about, lots of noise and chaos. No one knew what was going on or why this Tripper felt the need to wreck the place. There were no security personnel in the tech room at the time, and it would take them 3-5 minutes to show. At first, we tried calming him, well Rosa did, briefly. It was one of the funniest things I had ever seen. The Cajun had a tech in his arms and was using him to keep a clear swath around himself. Just kept swinging him around any time anyone tried to get near. So when Rosa went in to try and talk to Mr. Berserker Mode, she had to keep ducking every time the tech came swinging by her, all the while trying to get his attention and tell him it was gonna be ok. Talk about perseverance!" Grey looks over at Rosa admiringly, confident in her abilities, a good boss look.

"I found myself standing there for a second or two

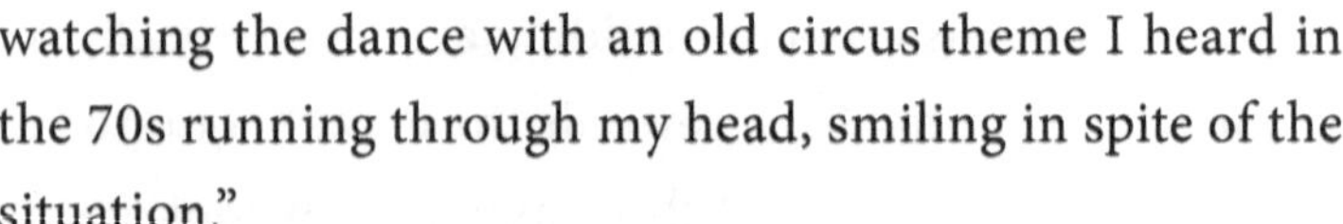

watching the dance with an old circus theme I heard in the 70s running through my head, smiling in spite of the situation."

"After a dirty look from Charles, I joined the fray! By this time, security was arriving and all hands on deck are needed to even attempt to strap him to a control board." A control board is similar to one used in medical situations to stabilize a victim's body in order to prevent further injury or harm. The control board is a tougher version used to prevent further injury or harm to people NOT being strapped to the board. "After a while we just started dragging the whole situation towards the doors and out into the hallway. It was just so comical that one dude stopped the entire process and wreaked that much havoc. I hadn't had that much fun in a long time!"

Laughing his ass off, Grey barely manages to continue, "All this time we are trying to strap him down and he keeps fighting out of it. By this time a couple of us were bashing him with pieces of equipment he had busted up when he was throwing shit at us, and the whole time he just kept saying the same thing. "Man, you mutha fuckas must be mad Te' plan' mad like a Cajun."

Rosa pipes in, "Remember what he said before he started tearing shit out of the ground? 'If you think you-a gonna git this badass from the swamps into that giant, warm, metal coffin, you can kiss zirable zinzin!'"

Miokel adds, "It was '*tete sure*' not badass. It means 'hard head,' I believe."

Rosa winks and says, "You can kiss zirable zinzin, know it all."

Grey continues, "As we regained control, or shall I say, managed to drag him out of the tech room and down the hall towards detention, I managed to get Charles' attention and said—" he starts laughing, "I said—"

Charles smiles profusely, "We definitely picked the right guy!" Both Charles and Grey go into almost uncontrollable laughter at their recollection to the absurdity of the moment.

Mackenzie, John, and June are pretty perplexed at the laughter at this point. Being in virgin territory and not battle or situationally hardened, they hadn't yet caught on to battle humor, or, as some call it, rescuer humor. Police, EMTs, doctors, and nurses all adapt to this type of humor in order to stay sane in repeated ridiculous, horrible situations.

But their time will come . . .

John inquests, "Since the badass Cajun went bonkers and you all bludgeoned him to death as he dragged you down the hallway," Grey gives him a look, continuing undeterred, "How did you get by the two body guards on the mission?"

Grey gives him a look like he should know.

Thinking, John comes up with nothing.

"We paid them off." Grey says.

John palms his forehead, realizing the obvious answer.

The laughter subsides slowly. It appears this was the perfect time for a good story. The team was deep in its pre-mission tension, and the story has moved them out of that.

CHAPTER FOURTEEN

G rey says, "OK!, enough of that. Does everybody have their part of the mission down? Any questions? No? Good! The other two teams can go."

Mackenzie, Miokel, Charles, and Rosa all grab their gear and head out the main door. Set in their mission, they don't look back.

"John and June, would you like to know what we are going to do?" Grey rhetorically asks. "We get the fun part."

Grey smiles in a way that really worries them.

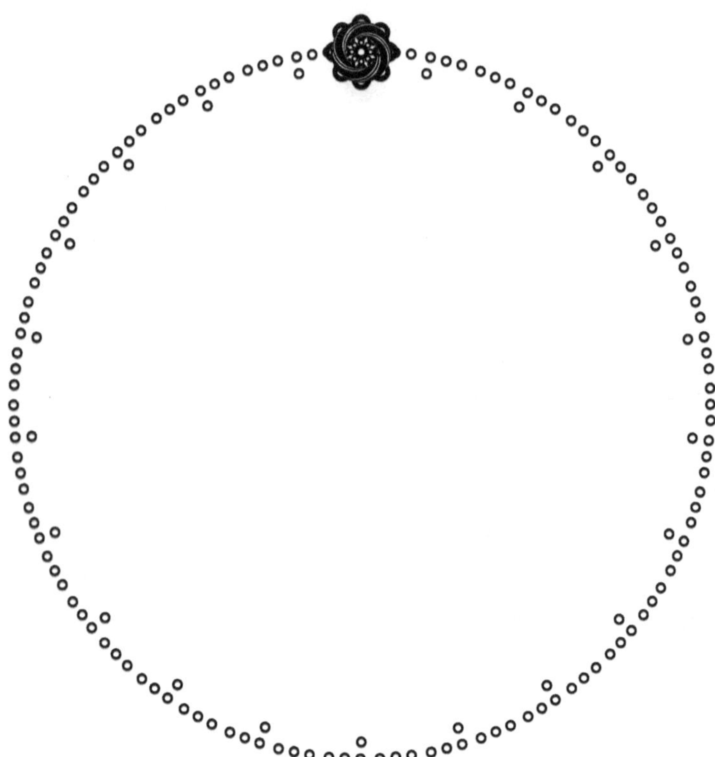

CHAPTER FIFTEEN

Having found themselves a great viewpoint on a hillside about 100 feet up in elevation from the target farm, Charles and Rosa scope out the scene below. The farm is located in a flat section of a valley surrounded by rolling hills, and mountains on the outskirts. A creek runs through the property just inside the first fence line and lots of old growth trees and orchards are contained within as well.

The buildings are grouped close together with a fence running between all the outer structures, creating an inner compound of sorts. Each building has an entrance facing this inner courtyard. Although each is sure to have back doors or secret escapes even, they still have a great line of sight from here.

Charles whispers to Rosa, "It is a pretty safe and hidden location. If it were a farm this would be a great

sustainable place to live; plenty of water, edge environments, and diversity. It surely was a farm at some point before being turned into a top secret facility some time during the cold wars."

Rosa not quite sure what he is talking about, just looks at him.

"What? I happen to be into Ecology!" he exclaims.

Rosa asks, "Seriously? With what you do for a living, you are into nature and shit?"

"Yes! Haven't you noticed, most former assassins are very Zen," smiling at her.

"Haha, actually, yes! Why is that?" Rosa asks.

"It has to do with balance. If we are just a warrior, we are out of balance. The artist, philosopher, and other things have to come into play in order to entice balance. The goal is to be a renaissance man of sorts. Not to mention, seeing way too many deaths puts a lot of things into perspective." Charles smiles genuinely.

"I can relate to that!" states Rosa humbly. In a quieter voice, "Ok, I guess we should be quieter; there are patrols about," she says and winks at Charles.

Both being of sound training and background, neither is oblivious to the fact that there is a patrol that runs not too far below them. The path below is not so obvious, nothing more than an animal trail but still visible to those in the know.

Suddenly they hear some noise below, off to their right. Rosa then smells the all familiar human scent, a mix of sweat odor, deodorant, and food. These guys smelled like processed foods, a mix of chemicals and sugar. Perhaps they are living off military rations with a side of candy. And something else. . .wait! Is that vanilla? Rosa rubs her hand back and forth across her nostrils trying to clear the smell. Vanilla? Really?

Regardless, they are headed this way and it is time to hunker down and get a first good look at who they will be dealing with, if necessary.

Charles and Rosa check their positions, looking behind them to make sure they aren't silhouetted by the sky or objects. Settling in on their haunches, they wait for the approaching guards.

The approaching guards are well armed, dressed in BDU type military clothing, and actually paying attention. Instead of chatting, they are silent and moving in a stealth mode, eyes ever-searching the hillside in front of them and the farm below. Moving quietly along the animal path, it is obvious these guys are mercenaries of some sort, hired hands to protect whatever was going on below.

Charles and Rosa watch the patrol, the farm below and everything else as well; there's not much going on. Then they catch a glint of light across the way, on the hill. Rosa shakes her head. Either Miokel or Mackenzie has a shiny object on them that is occasionally catching the sunlight. She just hopes the patrol is at an angle to not see it, or else Mackenzie and Miokel will be compromised. Now wishing they had a way to communicate live and wondering why if they had the technology to build an AED into their suit, why is it there are no communication devices created that are undetectable?

Looking over at Charles, she sees him looking from where he believes the patrol to be and back to where Miokel and Mackenzie are. At their current travel rates, it seems their paths will intersect in about ten minutes. If they don't find a good hiding spot before then, it might get interesting.

As Charles watches, suddenly the slow-moving reflection stops appearing. After a couple of minutes, still nothing. Charles is hoping and thinking they have found a good place from which to watch and observe.

Time will tell.

CHAPTER SIXTEEN

Miokel and Mackenzie arrive at an area that seems like it will suit their needs. It gives them good cover and provides a great view of the old farm compound below.

Compound seems a good word for it actually. As Miokel looks down, he notices the area around the buildings actually resembles one, there are fences and structures that provide a pretty secure area inside a hodgepodge of barns, sheds, fences, and livestock holding areas. None of the structures look new, but based on what Grey was saying, this may have been some cold war secret testing facility. God only knows for what, and God probably even doesn't want to know for what. Regardless, there is a great chance they will find everything they are looking for in bunkers or basements once they enter the buildings.

Scoping for guards and sentries, he sees none. This

worries him. Never wanting to assume the easiest possibilities, it means they are well hidden, out on patrol, or both.

Feeling Mackenzie fidgeting next to him, he gives her a look.

"I have to pee," she whispers.

"Didn't you pee yesterday?" he asks.

Mackenzie gives him the finger.

"I have to pee, like now!" she says, whispering loudly.

"It's been like six hours since we left our farm, I mean base, whatever. I . . . need . . . to . . . pee!" she says a little too loudly and startles herself. Hunching her shoulders she mouths, "Sorry!"

Resigned to the situation, Miokel motions for her to go take care of herself, to go pee.

Feeling like the rookie that she is, Mackenzie gets up and walks back towards some bushes they had passed, not far from their hiding spot. She keeps her head down and focuses on the bushes. She doesn't see the man approaching through some trees to her side. Stepping in front of her, startling her, he smiles.

Thickly accented he says, "Well, hello there, lovely."

She screams from surprise.

"I love it when I have that effect on people," he says, reaching for her. Having the complete advantage combination of surprise and size, he quickly subdues her in a brief struggle.

Hearing a scream and the struggle, Miokel curses himself for not paying attention to their surroundings while having a discussion on pee schedules! He stands up to go help Mackenzie and realizes he just screwed up again when he feels something rushing towards is head.

WHACK!

Unable to move in time, Miokel goes down from a blow to the back of the head.

Mackenzie is pretty pissed at herself for getting them caught, not so much for having to pee, which she still hasn't. The guard managed to get her to the ground without much struggle. With a knee in her back, she is at his mercy as he cuffs her hands behind her. Lifting her by them, she regains her feet. An even bigger guard approaches with Miokel over his shoulder; he lies there still as can be.

"Let's get these two back and secure them." he says.

"Ok," Mackenzies's guard says while grabbing her arm tighter. "She was an easy grab. No worries."

Shrugging his shoulder like there was a fly on it, he says, "This guy went down like it was his job!"

Both guards laugh at that.

"How is he?"

"He's a good one. He might be of some service to us." he says.

Instead of responding, the other guard grins mischievously.

Tightening his grip on Mackenzie's arm, the guard leads her down the path she and Miokel had just been walking on. After about 100 yards, he pulls apart some bushes and they descend a hidden pathway used as a shortcut to a gate located on the southeast corner of the compound.

Once there, the guard carrying the still unconscious Miokel uses a key pad to unlock the gate. They proceed straight to a barn and enter its side door.

Upon entering, Mackenzie notes nothing out of the ordinary and scans around the barn as they approach what appears to be a horse stall. Once they reach the stall, the guard pushes her forward, still commanding her with his grip. He moves her off to the side so the other guard can enter the stall with his Miokel package over his shoulder. The first guard slides the stall door causing a pulley system to lift a trap door in the floor of the stall. As the stall door comes completely closed, a concrete staircase is revealed below the wooden trap door.

When they reach the bottom of the stairs, the four proceed down a hall and through an unlocked door. Just beyond this door is a bench located near a drinking fountain with what appears to be a storage room across from it. The hallway continues with a couple more doors on the same side as the storage room and then ends at what appears to be another key-padded door.

Mackenzie's guard, using that iron grip, puts her

down on the edge of the bench, unlocks one of the cuffs, and after placing one end of the cuffs through the back of the bench, returns it to her wrist. Smacking her hard in the face for good measure, he then follows the other guard in through the storage room door and slams the door closed behind him.

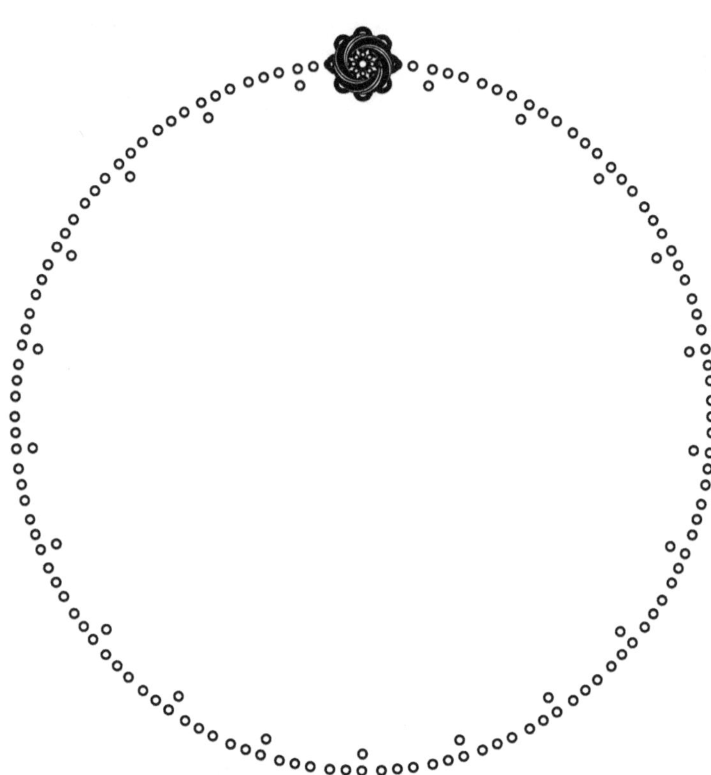

CHAPTER SEVENTEEN

Charles and Rosa watch the commotion, not that there was much, but to their watchful eyes they can tell what happened. Mackenzie and Miokel have been captured by the two patrolling guards that walked by them a few minutes ago.

Nothing happens for a couple of minutes, and then Rosa and Charles watch the group proceed down to the compound, entering through a southeast gate. From there they proceed to and enter a side entrance to a barn and are not seen again.

After about ten minutes, Rosa turns to Charles and says, "Well, should we go help them, or just stay and wait for Grey's arrival?"

Rosa knows the right thing to do in this situation, but is having doubts just the same.

"Tough choice, Rosa, we are supposed to stay and

observe everything up to and through their arrival. We are a backup plan of sorts at this point."

"But Mac and Miokel have been captured."

"Time to put your marine hat on Rosa. We will have to wait and get them later! Mission first, then no one left behind. I'll do what you say either way . . . you're in charge here, Ms. Dictator M'am."

Sighing, she knows he is right. Rosa hopes they are ok and knows Miokel can take care of himself; although he was carried in over one of the guard's shoulders!

"We wait," she says.

Making herself think about the big picture, she turns her energy instead towards the gate, willing Grey, John, and June's arrival. Miraculously, she hears an approaching vehicle.

Damn I'm good, Rosa thinks to herself. Settling back in, she gets ready for the next show.

CHAPTER EIGHTEEN

The guards slam Miokel down on the sorting table. Cold metal meets his cheek as it slams into his face. He starts to moan a bit and slowly move. His hands are pulled out straight in front of him and downward in an attempt to secure him to the table. Finding nothing convenient to lash him to, the guard chooses instead to add a rope and tie him to a deep utility sink located a little further back in the room.

In his haste, the other guard bellies up behind Miokel and pushes him against the table. He yells, "Fresh meat! I haven't had fresh meat in a while." Grinning, he pushes his groin up against Miokel's butt cheeks and grinds against them.

Finishing his task, the smaller mercenary saunters over, "Haha, me too, I can't wait. That damn scientist is getting boring. He's almost ok with it now!" He says, laughing and agreeing with the other guard.

Mackenzie sits dejected. Her hand secured to the bench, she strains to hear what is going on, on the other side of the thick door. Whatever it is, it can't be good. She has already heard some banging and yelling.

Focusing again at the task on hand, the guard behind Miokel tests his position. "Let's bring him up a little higher."

The other guard proceeds to adjust and retighten the hand rope around the sink. Confident of the wall's grip on the sink, the guard runs his hand along the rope as he approaches the front end of Miokel. Preferring a live, interactive experience, the guard slaps at Miokel's head a few times. With failure to elicit a response, the guard bangs on the table a few times, but still nothing.

He yells into Miokel's face, "Hey, you awake in there?" He gets nothing.

He bangs some more on the table and taunts, "Come out and plaaay." Still nothing.

The two guards look at each other.

Mackenzie hears the scuffling going on behind the storage room door: the meat-like sounds of impact to a human, the banging sounds. She knows they are beating Miokel, beating him because she had to pee. She is a failure. She has let her team down—1,000 percent unacceptable to her. She has to do something. She must!

She sees nothing around her to help her, nothing

she can turn into a magic key. Not that she can use to MacGyver anything, but she is looking for wire or something like it all the same. The hallway is clean and sterile, nothing but the bench ruins its uniformity.

"How hard did you hit him?" the smaller guy asks his bigger counterpart.

"Not hard at all actually, I was proud of myself. I hit him exactly where you would. Very accurate on the sweet spot." he defends.

"Instead of your normal brute force? Are you sure?" not so sure of his fellow hired hands conceptual awareness of his own strength.

Looking sheepish, the big guy shrugs his shoulders. "Lets just do him dry then. When he wakes, he'll tighten up!" Not waiting for a reply from his buddy, he grabs at what appears to be the meeting point between Miokel's pants and top, but his hand finds no purchase, it slides comically down through the area each time he tries.

Perplexing.

Miokel, who has been playing dead, springs into action. Feeling his feet barely touching the ground, he knows the time to act is now or he is fucked. . .literally. Bringing his knees up, he uses the table as support and drives his feet back, impacting his heels with the shins of the guard behind him; both legs snap to a straight position hyperextending one or both knees from the force.

The giant man behind him drops to his newly-arranged knees. The force of Miokel's action loosens the wall's grip on the sink. Managing to get his feet on the ground, Miokel pulls with his hands and scoots the table forward, allowing the guard behind him to fall to his knees in pain and causing more pain from the impact with the concrete. Before the guard can roll off his knees, Miokel brings his hands towards himself and twists at the torso bringing an elbow around and into the face of the guard already on his knees praying to his god for forgiveness. The man falls over backwards, hoping his prayer was heard as the lights go out for him.

The other guard wastes no time and brings a hard right fist down onto Miokel's head. Miokel doesn't see it coming and takes the full blow to the side of the head, causing him to bounce against the table. Wasting no time, the mercenary comes in to apply more damage. He brings up a knee, which Miokel manages to dodge, banging his head against the table in the process, which angers him even more.

Deciding to take it for a bit until he can find a good opening, Miokel lets the man land a few blows, managing to block all the power strikes or turn them into glancing blows. The guard grows weary as he attempts to pummel the tied-up Tripper into submission.

After landing several blows; he smiles with glee,

thinking he has this fucker right where he wants him. The mercenary puts both fists together into a giant hammer. Knuckles intertwined, he squeezes his hands together and brings them high above his head, the back of his prisoner's exposed neck his intended target. Instead, the tied up man grabs his leg behind the knee with both hands and heaves upward. All of his advantage disintegrates as he feels himself curving over backwards. He sees the ceiling and then the shelves and wall behind him as he involuntarily flips over backwards. Before he can do anything about it, his entire body slams against the concrete floor hard enough to make him bounce. The pain of the first impact registers as his body comes down again. The sound of hard bone and cartilage meeting concrete reverberates through his body. It aches, insane with pain.

Knowing it is life or death for him, the guard fights through it and forces himself to his feet.

Mackenzie, failing to find anything to help her get the handcuffs off, decides instead to do something more in line with her nature; she stands up and pulls hard on the cuffs, no budging. She yanks and jerks at them a couple times. The heavy bench barely moves, giving slightly. The cuffs? Nothing. No budging. No give. They have put the cuffs tight around her wrists.

Suddenly, Mackenzie puts one of her hands behind

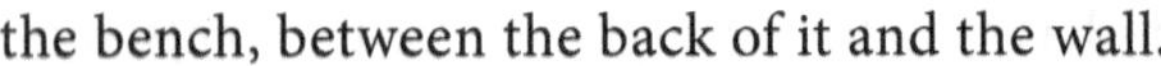

the bench, between the back of it and the wall.

Slam goes the sound of the bench hitting the wall.

Again, *slam*.

Slam, slam, slam!

She uses the weight of the bench to bash her hand, each and every blow causing more carnage; each and every *slam* increases the number of bone fragments in her hand. *Slam!* Knuckles pop and fingers shrink in length, the bones no longer able to keep them in place.

Mackenzie hears only the blood in her ears, the throb, throb, throb of her system as it sends blood rushing to her hand. She knows she has to pull now before all that blood reaches her wrist. Yanking hard she pulls her broken hand through the tightening metal structure of the cuff. It is easy to do now that her hand is entering shock and the pain receptors are on pause.

Feeling a rush of air, Miokel grabs at the other guard with his cuffed hands, expecting more fight. Instead the man heads for the door. Trying to catch him, Miokel is rebounded back by the constraints of the ropes, ending up on his back on the table causes it to screech its way across the concrete. Miokel rolls over backwards and lands next to the sink. Seeing the rope tied about the sink, he reaches for it and pulls as the guard reaches the door. The guard grabs the door handle and pulls it open fast and hard with intentions of fleeing for his life.

As she is standing up, the storeroom door opens inward. One of the guards is coming to see what all the ruckus is about. Meeting him at the door, Mackenzie brings her leg up and kicks him in the crotch as only a professional soccer player can. The driving force of her kick stops somewhere around his Adam's apple, bringing him to the ground in an instant heap. Stepping on and over him, she enters a room that has experienced some chaos. Miokel has obviously been putting up a fight.

Miokel is freeing himself from the ropes when she comes through the doorway into the storage room. Finishing his task he sees that Mackenzie has handled the fleeing guard. He immediately goes after the other guard, the one nearest him. Reaching down and grabbing him by the neck, he uses his cuffed hands as a latch to secure the mercenary in a prime bashing position. The guard who is basically unconscious is rocked off one wall and then a shelf and then the floor. Miokel brings him up one more time. The guard is again bashed against the wall, and with his cuffs still secure around his neck, Miokel brings him off his feet onto his back and slams him into the ground one final time. Angrily, Miokel brings his foot down on the man's face and neck area, driving his heel into the mercenary as he releases his anger at the attempted rape.

Mackenzie stands there in stone surprise. She has never seen this man release any real emotion, good or bad, since she first met him a few months ago. Deciding to let it play out, she watches in amazement as he moves from the one guard to the other. Almost out of steam he uses both feet to stomp on the already, mostly dead guard. Having gotten his anger out at the indecent proposal, he grabs his knife and finishes the job.

Slitting the throat of both guards for good measure, he then wipes the blade and returns it to his harness.

Mackenzie, standing there with her mangled hand, waits; but not for long because Miokel is a professional and professionals move on and heal quickly. He stands up, breathes deep and turns to Mackenzie saying, "Thank you for your help. See you might be up for this after all." Squeezing her shoulder he grins at her.

In spite of it all, she feels the need to smile; after all, they have escaped.

"Now what?" she asks.

"Mission onward. Let's catch up with Grey. I know where he is supposed to be." They pause long enough to remove the handcuffs from each other with a key they salvaged from a dead guard's pocket.

"Ok, let's go!"

They run down the hall and suddenly Miokel stops.

"Hey!" He points at a sign on one of the doors. It's a picture of a woman in a dress. On the door next to it is a similar silhouette without the world renowned triangle dress.

Mackenzie laughs and gratefully heads in the door.

When she comes out a few minutes later looking relieved, they continue down the hall, reaching the other key pad locked door.

Mackenzie says, "They used a code to get into the compound but not to get us to this point. Maybe we should go back the other way."

Miokel reaches for the key pad, and after only two attempts gets it right.

"How did you do that?" she exclaims.

"I woke up as we were coming down the trail and decided to ride the giant for a bit to see if we could gain access and information the easy way. Then they decided to try and ride me and that was the end of that."

Mackenzie realized what awakened the anger in her partner and said nothing, choosing instead to walk through the door and continue their mission.

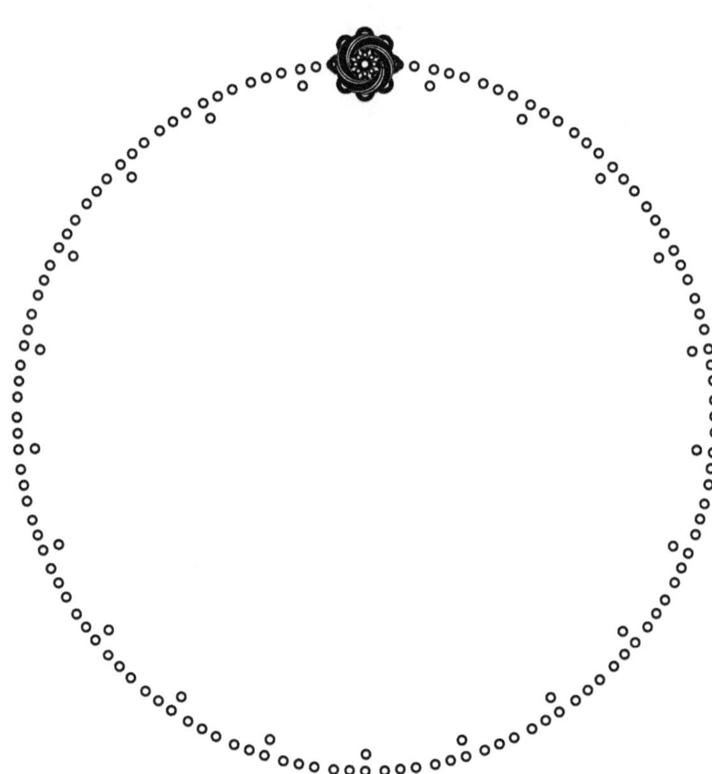

CHAPTER NINETEEN

June and John ride in the Zuk van while Grey drives. Grey insists the vehicle is from a so-called cold war about 20-30 years before the local time. But to June it is of alien technology, something from the monster movies of her time, brought down by aliens or created to fight the alien monsters that tried to end the 1950s as she knew it. Whereas John had the perspective that the cars of the 1950s, with their fins and chrome, were space ships disguised as cars. Listening to all this, Grey finds solace in John and June arguing about which was actually alien technology. He chose to abstain from the argument, not because he knows the truth, but because they were so engrossed in their conversation that he could see the nerves leaving their bodies. He wants them relaxed about their upcoming first action, well, first action of this type. He knows from their records that both have questionable pasts and experiences from living on the cracks and seams of society; a place only certain people are comfortable. Being one of those, Grey can pick them out in a crowd. He had thrived there long before being recruited into his current career. Current? He couldn't imagine doing anything else. It's like he was made to lead and travel to far realms.

Rounding a corner, Grey sees the farm rapidly approaching. John and June are still lost in their conversation, and an idea comes to him.

"Hey, guys!" They go silent.

"Sorry, Boss," John puts out.

"No, just the opposite actually. I think it will be a great idea for you two to keep talking and arguing while I deal with the gate and any possible gate guards."

June pipes in, "As opposed to just sitting here looking nervous and staring at the guard, hoping he can't feel me staring at him nervously?"

Grey nods his head as though to a beat from the strange song on the radio.

John gives her a look. "Do you always have to be right?"

She returns his look and they start up their banter again.

As they approach, Grey indeed does see an armed guard walk out from a garage like structure. He has apparently seen them approaching. Grey is glad he hadn't stopped for a pep talk once he saw the compound. That

would have seemed strange to the watching guard.

Slowing tremendously as they approach the compound, Grey notices the road drives along the fence for a bit before turning towards the gate. The guard motions for the vehicle to stop as he covers the ground between the garage and the fence. It appears he wants to talk through the fence before they reach the gate. Not the smartest way in the world to do it, but it works.

Grey slows to a stop while opening his window, John and June continue their banter unabated.

Back from the fence a few feet, weapon aimed at them, the guard sets the tone. "Why are you here?" he asks.

"We received a call to come handle some computer issues." Grey looks at a made up list located on a clipboard containing a work order of sorts: "Corrupt data, freezing up, and running slow is what it says here." Grey looks up at the guard, "Any more than that and you will have to ask the actual repairmen." He motions to the arguing techs in the vehicle with him.

"If they are the computer repairmen, why are you here?" addressing Grey.

"Same reason you are." Grey states in rebuttal.

The guard laughs and says, "Fair enough! I'll let the others know you are coming. Pull up to the main house and someone will meet you at the front door." Walking back to the garage, he hits a button located on the outside

wall. The gate slowly growls and clanks open as hidden motors and chains do their work.

Grey takes his foot off the brake and proceeds through the main gate area, driving the Zuk van the long way around the informal driving circle located in the center of all the buildings. He pulls up with the main house on the vehicle's right side and the van's distinct nose facing the main gate. You never know when you will need to make a quick getaway, after all.

A guard with an AK-47 slung over his shoulder exits the house through the main door and walks the porch to meet them. He has a stern, untrusting look on his face when John opens the door and exits the vehicle. June exits the vehicle behind him, and the guard's face turns to one of surprise.

"Hi," June says in her sweetest greeting voice.

The guard simply nods, his mistrusting mood realigned by her comforting style of being.

June continues, "We'll be out of y'alls way as soon as we can. Just let us grab some things and we'll get everything updated and running again as soon as possible."

The guard replies, "I didn't know anything was broken."

June touches him on the arm saying, "Well, honey, apparently somebody does. How about taking us to them, huh?"

"Sure thing ma'am, be happy to." he replies in his thick accent.

John and Grey's eyes meet in amazement at how quickly and easy it is for June to change the guard's demeanor. They grab the gear while June continues to chat with the guard. Walking the few steps onto the porch of the old farm house, they join June and the guard.

Grey humbles his face and body language, "We are ready when you are sir!" addressing the guard.

June hooks her arm through the guard's arm and, giving the impression of him leading, leads him through the door. "Lead the way. We can chat while we walk."

Forgotten by the guard who is completely enthralled by June, John and Grey follow in their wake. Taking a mental note of everything, they case the place as they move. Turning right, they walk through a living area into a working kitchen. Around the corner from the kitchen, the guard opens a door and they descend into a concrete basement. At first it has the appearance of a normal basement, junk and everything. If it weren't for the steel door with keypad located on the far wall, no one would be the wiser. Leaning against the wall near the steel door is a fake wall-piece of sorts. It was obviously intended to be placed over the door area. The amount of dust on it would lead one to believe that effort had been abandoned long ago.

The guard approaches the door, first removing June from his arm, leaving her a few paces back so she couldn't

see. He punches in the code, and the door springs open. Hearing the sounds, John deposits the code in his memory. He had no need to see; the keypad told him everything he needed to know.

Putting his arm out for June, the guard turns to the men trailing her carrying all the gear, "Close the door behind you. The scientists get freaky when we leave the door open, something about controlled environments." Turning back, he walks down the climate-controlled hall of the most sterile kind.

As they walk through the door, John obliges and pulls it closed behind him, noticing the click and the internal keypad as the door closes. Taking the time to point out to Grey the internal lock, they have to play catch up as June and the guard continue down the hall. The guard has apparently forgotten about them again.

Taking advantage of this, Grey lets his eyes wander about as they walk the well-lit, sterile hall. Deeper into the ground it carries them. At first the descent is unnoticeable, but after about thirty yards the hallway's declining angle increases and becomes apparent, so much so that handrails appear on the walls. The hallway continues to descend at a sharp angle for about another 100 yards. Grey notices that in its entire 130 yards there were no doors of any kind, no service entries or rooms. There are just a couple of air vents to keep those who walk it from

suffocating while walking from one end to the other. No doors and just a few small air vents made the distance and commitment into what some would call: a prime kill zone. Note to self.

Reaching the other end, the guard again remembers to leave June a few paces behind. The keypad sounds echo down the hallway leaving John no doubt as to the numbers needed to open this door also.

Following the guard through the door, they enter, if possible, a more sterile and brighter area than the hallway.

This one (once through the initial entry area) is full of scientific gear; some counters neat and in active use while others seem to hold gear in waiting or have the appearance of being used as desks. Upon first glance it would appear there are several work areas in the main room with several different projects in play, some encompassing glass containers with tubes running in between. Others hold dirt, soil, and plant life of several different stages and ages. There are two doors off the far side of the room. One of these appears to lead into a well-lit, glassed-in room. Plants are abundant there. The other door is windowless and key padded. It seems there is a lot to be seen and observed. They have hit the mother lode.

John looks about the room, seeking out the object of his affection. Looking around, he is starting to think it will be found elsewhere when he spots a back corner so dimly lit he almost doesn't see the computers resting there, waiting for his violation. Well, it's not violation but more like a caress. By the time they realize what is going on, it will be over. He will have milked them of all their goodness and information. They will tell him all he wants to know willingly, even beg for more and before they realize what is happening, he will be done. "Ahhhhhh," John sighs audibly earning a very inquisitive look from Grey. John shrugs, not wanting to apologize.

It's at this point that John sees the knife in Grey's hand. With the hilt in his palm and blade running along his wrist and arm, it was very hard to spot.

The guard ahead of them is totally engrossed in June, and happily walking her deeper into the room. June and the guard round a corner of sorts and head to one of the scientists for the introductions. John and Grey follow along. As they approach the corner, Grey using the case in his right hand, moves John back a bit and takes the lead. He has been sizing up the situation since they entered the room. Long ago trained in clearing rooms and endowed with acute situational awareness, Grey spotted the awakening guard as soon as they entered the room, the glass in the far wall reflecting lots of pertinent information.

John sees the legs of a stool appear out of nowhere as they approach. Just as surprisingly, he witnesses Grey's left hand come up and hammer fist an unlucky guard in the

face. Gracefully, Grey places his case on the ground and tilts the stool back onto its hind legs in one clean, swift, quiet movement. Removing the knife from the guard's eye allows his head to return to the napping position, permanently this time. Grey takes him out before he can plant all four stool legs on the ground, no one the wiser.

Not 100% surprised as to what just happened, John scoops up Grey's case with his other hand, leaving Grey free to do what he pleases, unencumbered. The cases were John's part of the deal anyway.

Grey approaches June and the guard in her arm.

There are three other men in the room. All appear to be scientists: the one June and the guard are approaching and two others doing their own thing in different areas of the room. Depending on how this plays out, Grey may have to go loud. Pulling his hidden pistol and firing it before finding out if there is anyone else within earshot would be disappointing and potentially very dangerous. He decides to see how this plays out.

Looking up from his work, the scientist looks perturbed. "What's going on?" he addresses the guard and glances over at June. Even he and his distracted mind pause and check her out. There is an intelligence in her eyes; he sees it instantly. And how could you not? A depth and a lost soul deep in there wanting to get out. He could relate to that.

June bats her eyes and gives her best greeting, "Hiii." The scientist's heart skips a beat in spite of things.

Addressing the guard directly, he asks, "Seriously, why are they here?" using an arm motion to address the lab, "and why are they in my lab? No one is allowed in here. You know that! You guys are becoming anti-productive. I'm going to have to do something about this!"

The guard is taken aback and says, "They said you called them here to fix the computers. I know the computers are important to you so I brought them down to you." Pausing, he adds, "They came all this way."

The scientist replies, "Exactly! Why would someone come all this way uninvited?" looking at June accusingly.

At this moment Grey appears next to the scientist, drawing his attention from the guard to his own giant stature. Initially staring at Grey's chest, the scientist takes a step back to be able to look up over the giant man's beard and make eye contact with him. "And who are you? You are here to steal my stuff, are you not?" Grey admires his confidence for a second before responding.

Grey asks him, "Are you Professor Nowak?"

Looking shocked, the scientist takes a step back, "You are here to steal from me!" is his reply.

At this point, the guard removes his arm from June's and looks at her angrily. He starts to unsling the AK-47 from his shoulder, not saying anything.

June pleads with him, "No, it's not what you think."

"Yes it is!" the scientist shouts at the guard. Looking through all the people gathered around him, he addresses the sleeping guard. "Do something!" There's no movement from him. By this time the other two scientists are aware something is up and are paying attention. Their work on pause, they stand and watch from their work stations aghast, seemingly what they feared the most is happening. Hands holding the implements of their trade, they stand frozen.

The guard manages to get the rifle sling off his shoulder, but Grey is there in an instant and takes him out with an elbow to the temple before he can even find the trigger. Grey lets the guard unceremoniously fall to the ground as he turns back to face the scientist.

Unaccustomed to what she assumes is death, June steps back. Gasping in horror, her hands come to her face. She can't help but stare at the guard lying on the floor. In her previous career, death was not on the menu. The grifters she ran with didn't kill; they lied, cheated, stole, and used their wiles to get what they wanted. Instant death is new to her.

Grey turns around just as the lead scientist is grabbing for some glass objects. The work area is full of long and cylindrical vials and beakers containing various liquids. The scientist proceeds to grab a tall, half-full

one and swings it towards Grey. Grey uses his knife arm to block it, and it shatters instantly against his arm. Not even pausing for effect, the scientist grabs for another one. Not wanting to kill the scientist, Grey moves in to subdue him. He sheaths the knife in its hidden location under his sleeve with a simple flick of his fingers. Quicker than he looks, the scientist manages to grab another liquid-filled cylinder and swing it at Grey. Grey being even faster, manages to grab the man's wrist this time, causing the object to release from his hand and bounce off Grey before smashing and shattering at ground level.

One of the scientists flees for the far, key-padded door. It is at this moment that the door starts to open. Unaware, he grabs the door and pulls just in time to help Miokel enter the room. Miokel applies a forearm shiver as a thank you for his assistance. The scientist, unaccustomed to such actions, crumples to the floor, maybe someday to wake up and start to contemplate what happened. Miokel notices this is twice today that he and Mackenzie have had perfect timing when it comes to doors.

Mackenzie follows Miokel through the door, mangled hand held tight against her belly. The arm is starting to throb, but she has willed through pain before. She will be okay. Looking about the room she sees everything seems to be progressing nicely. June stands looking at someone lying on the floor who seemed to be a guard.

There appears to be another guard sleeping deeply on a stool tilted against a wall. She steps over the unconscious scientist at her feet and looks up just in time to see John bowl another scientist over with a case as he is heading for a far door. Mackenzie marvels at his form as he slides the case at the calves of the fleeing scientist; leg kicked out to the side, arm follow through and everything. Grey is in the middle of the room, getting the best of another scientist. It seems she is not needed to fight at this point. She goes to help remove June from her shock.

Quickly gaining control of the scientist, Grey spots some ancient numbers tattooed on the scientist's arm. He realizes that the one person in the room who had yet to be knocked out or killed was indeed the one he was hoping to take home with them. "Aha, you are the man I am looking for. Hello, Mr. Nowak."

Still struggling, the professor manages to grit out between his teeth, "That's Professor, you ape!"

Grey manages to turn the professor around and force him against the work table. By this time, Miokel has reached them and helps hold the professor down.

Looking about the room, Grey takes stock of the situation. All seems to be in order. The only unknown was the window-filled side room. "Mackenzie, go look through those windows and make sure we are squared away." She points at the sleeping guard in response. Grey

smiles, "Don't worry about him. He's a non-issue."

All else seems to be in order.

"John!" He looks back at Grey and says, "Go do your thing." Grey motions with his head towards the computer corner.

After retrieving the other case, John heads to the computer corner. Arriving with eyes hungry, salivating even, he caresses the ancient computer of old. Running his hand across the separate computer monitor, he marvels at its thickness and stereotypical dirty-cream color finish. He rounds the desk and looks under it to locate the rectangular box they used to call "the computer." Sitting in the chair, he settles in for his work. "This should be easy." he says to no one in particular. He can get the mother board and memory chips out with no problem. He just might need help locating any back-up disks. Chuckling, he wonders if they could be on one of those 3 ½-inch floppy disks!

Having found the windowed room free of human beings and full of nothing but plants, Mackenzie returns to comfort June, while Grey and Miokel secure all three scientists with cord they acquired from various electrical devices in the room. The two seemingly dead guards are left where they lay, trussed up just the same.

With Miokel and Mackenzie present in the room, Grey knows that Rosa and Charles are out on overwatch.

They will without a doubt handle any new arrivals to the compound. Part of their previous instruction is to not allow additional entry once Grey and his team arrived.

Not sure if there are any more guards inside the buildings, he and Miokel push some heavy tables against the two keypad doors so John can work in peace.

Grey glances over at John to make sure he is working. He spies him caressing and talking to one of the computer boxes just before taking a powered screwdriver to one of its screws.

Grey nudges Miokel, "John seems to have an inappropriate relationship with computers. We may have to keep an eye on him."

Having noticed this as well, Miokel laughs out his response. "I know! Right man for the job, huh?" After a short pause he asks, "Now what, Boss? Are we just waiting for John or are we on the hunt for more scientists?"

Grey responds, "No more hunting. We have found the scientist we are looking for. He is the only mandatory human. To be honest, the remaining two are up to him. Does he want to bring them with us or leave them here? John will have to verify that the information we are looking for is on the computers and then we are out of here."

Miokel adds, "So we are on hold until the information is verified? There's no reason to start a conversation with the lab nerds until then."

"I agree." Grey is grateful to have Miokel's brain in these situations.

Curious, Miokel watches John work. John is removing components from the computer boxes and placing them into a receiving slot of sorts located in one of the cases they brought with them. After a moment, he removes it and then places another in the same slot.

Miokel nudges Grey, "What is he doing now?"

"Verifying the information we want is on the drives and disks he finds. Even John doesn't know what exactly we are here for. You and I learned a long time ago to not be curious, but others may be. So the techs came up with the device in the case to read the information on the computer. It simply gives John a red or green light. If it's green, the hard drive goes, if the light turns red it is of no use to us."

Miokel considers this and finds it interesting, "It seems all information would be valuable."

Grey nods in agreement and then addresses Miokel, "Hey, what happened to Mac's arm by the way?"

Miokel, looking a little sheepish responds quietly, "I screwed up, Boss. She had to pee, and I didn't clear the area before she got up to handle it. We were ambushed and taken here," nodding towards the door he and Mackenzie entered through. "They isolated us."

Grey asks, "Who's they?"

"Two guards—now handled." Continuing his story,

"They left her handcuffed to a wooden bench in the hall and took me into a supply closet. She heard the commotion and according to her, bashed the bench against the wall to break her hand after quickly trying other things."

Grey's only response is a raise of the eyebrows.

"That's hardcore, Boss. Can we keep her?" Miokel looks at Grey like he is asking to keep a rescue from the pound.

"Absolutely!" He pauses and adds, "And I think I just figured out her cherry gift." Before Miokel could ask what it was, Grey walks away to check John's progress.

Walking up to John, Grey asks, "How's it coming John? Are we about ready to go?"

John puts the last drive in the checking device. He gets a red, pulls the drive and chucks it over his shoulder. "Done, that was the last one. I don't know why these scientists kept bad computer drives."

Grey had wondered what the techs told John about the checking device, and now he has a good idea. "Do you know if we have all the information we are looking for?" Grey asks.

John looks at the device in the case. There are four rows of green lights, all lit up. "The lights seem good to go. The techs back, um . . . home, told me when all four green lights were lit up, we are copasetic; and they are lit." John gathers up his things, "What's next? Are we headed out of here?"

Grey answers, "I think so. We just need to see how

many of these brainiacs are coming with us."

Grey gives Miokel the thumbs up so he can get everyone ready to go. He then walks over to the lead scientist and whispers quite a bit into his ear. A look of shock crosses Professor Nowak's face. Recovering, he whispers back at Grey. Grey looks at him, nods in agreement, and walks towards his crew.

Addressing all his crew he says, "Good thing we brought a big vehicle. All three scientists are coming with us. Let's keep them tied and secure until they are out of our hands." Addressing the three rookies he reminds them, "It's always a good idea to keep our cargo secure and under control until it or they are out of our hands, too many variables . . ."

"Ok, let's continue with the action plan. Our van is parked at the front porch located through that door." Grey points at the door beyond the sleeping guard. "It's about a two minute walk." Grey addresses Miokel, "Is your way shorter?" A shake of the head is his only response.

"Then John and June, you go first and be prepared to schmooze anybody that appears. We will just need you to buy us a few seconds if we do run into anybody. I can take it from there."

June's skin flushes a hot red. She has a good idea what he means. She heads for the door, intending to be the first person with hopes of handling any situations with-

out more death involved.

John, hot on her heels, tightens his grip on the two cases and gets ready for anything. Liking his new gig, he is ready to put on a show for his new boss. Carrying out the two heavy cases is his way of showing his resolve. Besides, he would rather let Miokel and Grey do the other grunt work at this point. Dealing with humans wasn't his forte . . . yet.

June is through the door, John is forced to hurry and throw a shoulder against it to stop it from slamming shut. Thankfully, Miokel appears and grabs the door ready to hold it for those remaining so John can catch up with June.

Grey walks out of the lab area and into the hall. The scientists walk behind him, hands tied but of free will just the same. Grey saw the Professor whispering to the other two scientists a few moments ago and is pretty sure by their behavior that he passed on the words Grey said to him; therefore, he had buy-in from them.

As long as they didn't run into anyone on the way out, this would go smoothly.

All in the hallway now, Miokel, the last to leave, closes the door behind him. Waiting for him, Mackenzie sees him lean over and place something between the door and the jam, preventing it from clicking tight.

He and Mackenzie walk behind the others up the slowly rising sterile hallway. The trip through the base-

ment, up the stairs and back around to the front of the farmhouse is tense, every corner an unknown. Yet the kitchen and living room are empty and void of noise. The Zuk van sits out front waiting patiently; as is June, who is standing just inside the front door. Not knowing if it is wise to go outside yet, she waits for all to catch up.

Due to the limited space, the group ends their forward movement stacked in the living room. All seem to glance outside upon arrival, except Mackenzie. She stands and looks at the scientists. They don't seem that bad, yet her hand still feels the effects of their protection. After that moment almost an hour ago, she thought for sure the rest of this day would be full of terror and violence. Instead, she stands there watching three pasty scientists look out the window to see if it was raining or not. This job is going to be interesting for sure.

Grey, having seen what he needed to see out the window says, "Thanks for stopping, June. All looks good outside. Upon my mark we will casually head for the vehicle. The three scientists will be loaded in the back. John and June will take the same seats as before. If the gate guard thinks all is good, then we are home free."

"Can't we just take him out? It might be easier," Miokel suggests.

"Yes, but we have a plan he could help out with if we can leave him breathing." All look at Grey inquisitively, especially the scientists. "Rosa will fill us in later," he adds, deferring the team's questions and leaving the scientists confused.

"Ok, June, we are ready when you are." Looking at her, he smiles at her reassuringly.

She hesitates for only a second and then pushes open the door. Resuming her persona, she walks towards the van and opens the side door so John can place the cases inside. Instead, he steps into the van with them in hand, an efficient tactic for sure. Close on his heels, the scientists follow him into the van and find places on the floor to sit. Miokel follows and assists Mackenzie into the van. They both sit cross-legged on the floor with the scientists.

Having walked around to the driver's side, Grey enters and starts the van while June climbs into the passenger seat. Starting right up, Grey puts the van into gear, pauses for a breath, and realizes he hasn't communicated with Rosa and Charles. Putting the van back in park, he climbs back out and walks to the back of the van. Grey motions towards where he knows Rosa and Charles are watching from. He puts his left hand in the air, arm outstretched, and moves it in a circular motion setting a specific action plan into motion. They have been given previous instruction and will be on clean up. He also signals to them an idea of what they will find: four bodies, one live armed

human (possibly more), and some Tripper DNA to handle. Knowing those two, he walks to the van totally confident they will succeed. Chuckling, he is thinking they may even get back before the van group. A couple klicks' hike over rolling mountains and a dirt road drive all the way around the range—he wouldn't bet money on beating them there, such is his confidence level.

The gate guard, way overdue for his nap, paces back and forth inside the garage area. Not wanting to be caught asleep when the computer techs try and leave, he is up and pacing about the place to stay awake. A creature of habit, his body fights with him to lie down on the garage couch, if only for a minute. His mind knows his boss will commence beating on him if he does sleep while the visitors are here, so he waits anxiously for the sound of their vehicle.

Thankfully, after what seems like forever, he hears the van start up. Instantly cheerful, he heads outside to hit the button. Coming outside as the van enters into motion, he pushes with his finger on the push button located on the wall. The gate starts moving with its normal groans and clanking. Moving surprisingly fast, it is ready when the van arrives.

Looking into the front of the van, the guard waves lightly at Grey and June, and receives a two finger wave from Grey and a big southern wave from June on their

way out. With his other hand already on the close button, he pushes it as soon as he thinks the van is far enough through the gate. Not waiting to see, he heads around the side of the garage to empty his bladder before napping. He hears the gate scrape the rear bumper of the van as it narrowly escapes the closing gate. Pausing for a second to see if he is going to catch some hell, he hears the van instead accelerate and zoom away. Breathing a sigh of relief, he returns to his current mission of relieving his bladder; sometimes the best feeling in the world. . .well, maybe tied with a good nap. He is eager to finish, as one is a prerequisite to the other.

As soon as they are clear of the compound, John gives up his seat. Miokel helps Mackenzie climb into the seat, injured arm now held against her body with a hasty sling fashioned from a cut-up lab coat. He motions to John to come closer so he can whisper in his ear. "I want you to sit in back with the scientists. Keep an eye on them, and shout out if they try anything stupid." John looks at him inquisitively, "You know, like untying themselves and trying to dive out the back door, stuff like that." John nods in acknowledgement and says, "Got it."

Mackenzie, now sitting behind Grey, leans closer to him and asks, "What about Rosa and Charles?"

"They have some work to do and will be joining us later."

Mackenzie had several thoughts as to what "work they had to do" but decided it was best to keep it to herself for the moment. She instead settles back into the van's seat and relives the past couple of days. The past couple of years even come into her mind. Who knew life could change so much in a short period of time? Somehow, she had gone from soccer star to being charged with manslaughter to being recruited for this new, exciting career as a Tripper. She doesn't know what the future will bring. She just knows this new gig is a great adventure and way better than being imprisoned for bludgeoning to death the man who had so gratuitously betrayed her trust by sleeping with as many other women as possible, up to and including her teammates. She also knows that although she needs to work on her anger issue, it sure came in handy today. Rubbing her arm and feeling the swelling along with the numbed pain (from shock), she longed for some good pain killers and a stogie, hopefully consumed just before a long, hot, post-game shower.

Almost like magic, Miokel's hand appears in front of her with two tiny oblong pills in his hand. "Here," he says, "you can have these now. It will help with the pain and swelling a bit without turning you into a zombie. You'll get the zombie tabs back home."

"Zombie tabs?"

"Yep! You place them under your tongue, and they will put you out for a few days. By the time you wake up out of it, your arm will be healed. The benefits of today's medicine for sure. We call them zombie tabs because they knock you the fuck out!" He grins at her, "You will wake up in your quarters drooling on yourself with no recollection of the last few days."

"Hmmm, sounds good and bad to me." she says.

Miokel reaches up and grabs her good arm for a second, "You did good today. It was me who fucked up and didn't have your back. It won't happen again."

The look on his face told her everything she needed to know.

She smiles down at him, a look of appreciation envelops her face . . . that's all she really wants, people to have her back like she has theirs. Resting back against the side of the van best as she can, she closes her eyes, relieved to have found the kind of people for whom she has been looking. They are the kind who are in it as much as she is.

Despite the lack of zombie tabs, she still manages to sneak off to sleep.

Noticing this, Miokel settles back onto his haunches. Ready to shut down for a couple minutes himself, he closes his eyes. Hearing nothing but the engine, the tires on dirt, and John starting up a banter with the scientists, he allows himself to hit the recharge button.

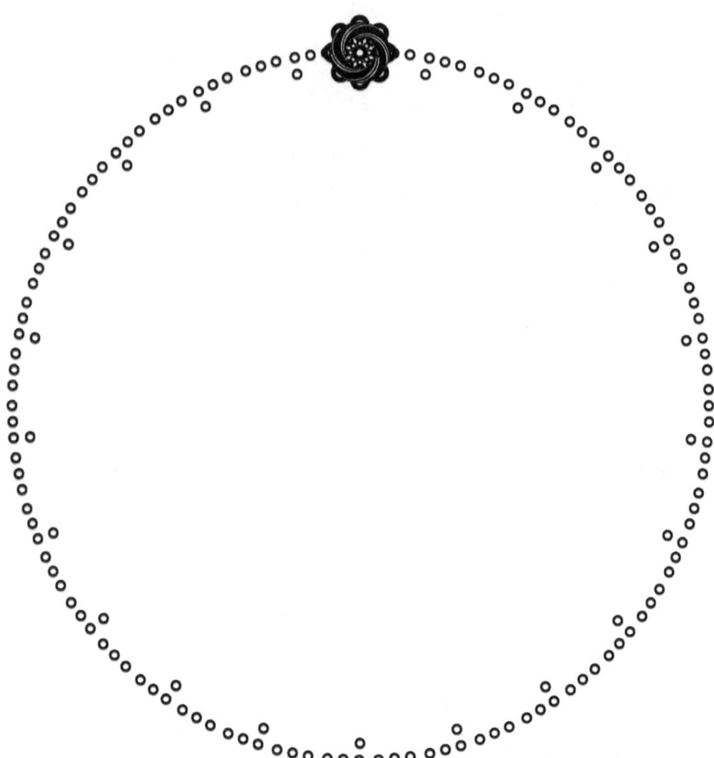

CHAPTER TWENTY

osa and Charles watch the nothing below; all is still. Since Grey and the team's arrival, nothing has moved within the compound. They have not seen the two guards who entered the barn with Miokel and Mackenzie, or the guard stationed in the garage for gate duty.

Both having been in this business (in one shape or form) for a very long time, they wait patiently with little effort, for something to happen. It has merely been an hour since the team entered the house, not that long in the scheme of things. They are both aware of the strong possibility that the buildings are just a facade and there is probably a vast complex underground.

Charles is more accustomed than most to the "sit and wait" business. Most assassins spend a decent amount of their quality time observing and planning. It is something that must be inherent in their nature to succeed. I mean, how can an impatient person sit for hours to watch and learn a person's patterns in order to find the best way to take them out? Of course, there is more than one type of hit-man on the planet. Some do go in with guns blazing, making it up as they go along. They just don't require any retirement planning.

Charles rubs his temples with his thumb and middle finger. Although his nature is introverted and patient, his brain has still managed to fill with images and demons. He is mostly successful at keeping them tidy in nice, tiny, solid, leak-proof boxes in his brain. It is only when he lets down his guard, and allows his brain to relax that they come out to haunt him. Usually, this happens when he sleeps. Putting his hand on his pocket he relaxes sub-consciously; glad to have found a way to combat that from happening. Sleep does the body good after all. He's a 1,000 times better now that he's figured out a way to sleep. Who knew that getting high on marijuana would help him sleep? Back in his day only the hippies and Vietnam veterans were smoking it. The hippies to alter their minds, and increase their peace, love and other, what do they call those . . . feelings? yah, that's it.

The veterans, well they probably smoke it for the same reason Charles does; to shut off his mind so it will let him sleep, keep the committee in his head at bay, and

the horrors safe and secure in their tight little boxes.

It's amazing that in the 1960's and 70's version of the United States, marijuana was considered a recreational drug for lazy people, and in 2114 his therapist hand delivers his medical prescription of marijuana. She hand delivers a few other things too, but that is a story for another day.

He hears movement down below as Rosa nudges him. They both watch as the rest of the team walks out of the farmhouse nonchalantly like they have just been visiting Grandma. If it weren't for the three dudes in lab coats with their hands apparently tied in front of them, no one would know any different. They watch the team load into the small van like experienced circus clowns as Grey walks around to the driver's side and gets in. He starts up the engine and put his foot on the brake ready to go.

Rosa's brain starts to wonder just as she sees the brake lights go off and Grey depart the driver's side to walk to the backside of the van. He looks in their general direction, and using hand signals tells her everything she needs to know prior to heading down to leave behind a story to be detected later.

Rosa brings Charles up to speed, "They took out four people. The guard at the gate may be the only remaining witness but not sure about that! So we should be ready just in case."

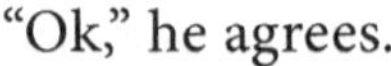

"Ok," he agrees.

"How do you think we should go in?" she asks him.

"You tell me," he throws back at her, "it's your show." Grinning at her mischievously, he awaits her command.

Formulating her thoughts, she comes up with a plan. "Let's go in through the barn. It's closest to us and there is no chance the gate guard will see us. I don't know when he will become suspicious that something has gone down. So, quick-and-quiet is my plan. If we can get out of here undetected he can help sell the story."

Charles nods in consensus.

"Would you like me to go first?" he asks her.

"Go for it, hon." She replies.

Barely leaving his crouch, Charles works his way down the hill and to the compound. Heading around the outside of the fence, they find their way to the gate. Listening first, he then opens the gate slightly and listens again. Stealthily, they close the gate and head for the side of the barn. Entering, they pause to let their eyes adjust.

They notice nothing peculiar about the barn. Between them, they scope the entire building. Finding nothing they stand in the middle to confer.

Rosa does the talking and says, "I find nothing. You neither I take it?" He shrugs his shoulders and opens his hands in agreement. "There must be a hidden passageway here somewhere. Otherwise Mackenzie and Miokel

wouldn't have come out of the house like they did."

"Perhaps we go to the house and see what we find there. It's just next door," Charles offers up. "We can always come back here and try again if need be."

Perking up, she commands, "I like it. You lead the way."

Charles heads back out the door they entered through. It brings them out near the gate located between them and the farm house. Choosing to move along the fence, he uses it as cover. Looking off towards the front gate and garage, he sees no movement. He continues along the fence and brings them around to the backside of the house. Pausing for a sound check and hearing nothing, he beelines for the back door. Again hearing and seeing nothing, he pulls open the door and enters the house. Rosa follows.

Finding himself in the kitchen of a farmhouse, he spots an open door in a hall just off the kitchen. He sees descending stairs and points them out to Rosa.

Rosa whispers, "Let me check this floor first." Thinking about how much it would suck to descend into the basement just to be surprised from someone above, she wants to make sure this floor is clear.

Charles stands against the wall listening and waiting. He could hear Rosa clear the remaining parts of the house. Quickly and efficiently he hears her go room to room, opening all doors she comes to. Next thing he knows she is standing beside him having made a complete circle of the house.

She nods the all clear to him.

Without hesitation he descends into the basement. Scoping the area around him he quickly notices the steel door on the opposite wall. Approaching it he finds it slightly ajar, held open by a piece of basement junk. Rosa positions herself to the far side of the door. When she is ready, Charles opens it. Looking first, she quickly enters the long hallway. With Charles close on her heels, they quickly cover the distance to the door located at the other end of the long, sterile, well-lit hallway.

Arriving at the other end of the hall, she notices someone has stuck a notebook in the door so it wouldn't be able to close all the way. Seeing the keypad lock, she is grateful for the time-saving action.

When Charles is ready, she pulls the door open with one hand and grabs the notebook with the other. She doesn't want it to fall and create an echo throughout the basement.

Entering the room, Charles sees they have found the area they are looking for. Hearing Rosa enter behind him, he moves to the left while she moves right around the room.

The first thing that grabs Charles' attention as he moves about the room is the sleeping guard still tipped back

on his stool. Charles, like Grey, first spots him through the glass reflection. Pretty sure this guy was handled, he approaches with caution just in case. As he rounds the corner, the congealing fluids that escaped the guard's eye onto his belly make it obvious. Someone had laid a perfect strike to the man, killing him instantly; which is a great, painless death, Charles thinks to himself.

They continue through the room, look into the grow room and continue to the far key padded door. He and Rosa meet.

"Well, we are definitely here," she states.

Motioning with her head she says, "The guy in the middle is done from a blow to the head. The other guy, too?"

"Yah, but from a sharp object to the eye. Must've been Grey or Miokel who applied it based on the precision."

"Ok, there's not much DNA here. Grey said there was some Tripper DNA somewhere. We have to find it and neutralize it just in case the blast doesn't handle it."

Charles smiles at her, knowing they are about to blast this place to smithereens.

"Let's go ahead and find it, then we can come back here."

He nods in agreement.

Making eye contact, he places his hand on the door, and she nods to go ahead and open it.

As he does, she peeks through the increasing opening. Quickly moving in and down the hall, she sees the bench askew in the hall and a body at its feet. The body holds open a door, appearing to lead to a storage room. She works her way down the hall, pointing at Charles and the two restrooms; they are his to clear. She reaches the body on the floor, holding the door; upon closer inspection she confirms this is the other area they are looking for.

Charles catches up to her, having paused to apply the notebook trick to the other key padded door, and clear the two bathrooms on the way. He sees the body at her feet, and enters the room through the doorway the dead man so graciously held open for him.

Upon entering, the nature of the room becomes apparent, as does the commotion that went on here; the big metal table at an odd angle, the blood on the floor, and the sink violently removed from the far wall are dead giveaways that a struggle of some sort occurred here. The two guards are dead giveaways as to the victor.

Rosa breaks the silence and says, "I can't wait to hear this story." She raises her eyebrows and smirks at Charles.

"I know, right? What happened here wasn't as smooth as the other room. This must be where the DNA is located." Looking around, he spots numerous cleaning agents, some surely to contain ammonia or bleach, which are both good contaminators of DNA. You just have to pick one. You don't want to mix those two ingredients together!

Rosa, spotting them as well, formulates a short plan.

"Go ahead and do what you can to contaminate the DNA. I want to scope out the rest of this hallway. There is another door at the end, I want to see where it goes."

"Cool," is his only reply.

Bellying-up to the shelving units as she walks away, he quickly finds a couple of options to use. Figuring more is better in this particular case, he grabs a couple of different jugs of what appears to be strong cleaning agents. A feeling of dread washes over him as he glances at the labels, not recognizing the language on it. He knows enough that mixing certain chemicals used in cleaning agents causes toxic gases and, not wanting to die today, he decides using all of the same type of cleaning agent is a good idea. Both have the international (and apparently time-honored) skull and crossbones. Not sure what to do, he decides to go with the one with the most warning labels.

He places the other back on the shelf and grabs another container of his chosen cleaner. He brings the bottles to the table to remove the caps. He picks both up again, one in each hand. Charles pours the solution over the metal table and then proceeds around the room pouring as he goes. Focused on being overly thorough, he pours the cleaner over the rope on the floor, the sink torn from the wall, all over the floor, and the body lying there.

Having emptied the first two containers, he grabs two more and repeats the process at the table. He then walks into the hall, pouring as he goes, ensuring to cover the body holding the door open for him. He finishes up by covering the bench and the two sets of cuffs that sit there with the liquid.

Pausing for a second, he has a thought and flips over the body on the floor with his foot. Rolling the body towards the door it opens a little further. Charles pours the cleaner over the areas that were just a second ago protected by the body, up to and including the front side of the corpse. He then does the same procedure on the other unlucky guard.

As he finishes he feels Rosa's return and turns to her in the doorway, "All done here." he says.

"Good!" she continues, "We never would've found it."

"Found what?" he asks.

"Well, I shouldn't say never, but it would've taken a while." While motioning with a thumb over her shoulder, she says, "The door at the end of this hall goes up a flight of stairs and into the barn through a trap door in the floor. The trap door opens from above by closing the door of the horse stall that contains it. It would've taken us forever to find it. I was able to push it open and climb through to figure it out."

"Pretty cool," is his stone-faced reply.

She can't tell if he is not impressed or if it's just the normal Charles nonchalant demeanor.

As if an answer, he throws the jugs back in the closet. "What's next, Boss?" he smiles at her.

Already having the plan, she tosses him what is affectionately known as a "sidbe-one," or officially: a S.D.B.B.-1. There are three levels of this particular device. She brought several level 1s and level 2s just in case they were needed. Being the over-prepared type, she longed to have a S.D.B.B.-3 with her, but didn't want to do the approval paperwork. Apparently the S.D.B.B.-3s were "too explosive," whatever that means. Therefore, one needed to obtain approval from the lead Tripper and his CO in order to obtain one from the armory. Deciding to skip the red tape, she just brought more than even she thought was needed of the smaller two.

Looking at the device he caught in his hand, Charles smiles. Always a fan of big explosions, he is joyful of her decision.

Rosa lays out her plan, "I'll go back to the lab area and set one up. Between this," she shows him the one in her hand that appeared to be a level two, "the lab gasses, and fertilizer located in there, it will do the job. Set yours for ten minutes. It should give us plenty of time to find a nice viewing position."

"Why don't we just use the remote?"

"Because it leaves a traceable signal, remember?"

Smiling at her, he nods in agreement. She walks away,

instantly excited at her next task.

He looks down at the device in his hand. About the size of a tube of Mentos mints, it is mostly one solid piece. The last third of one end has the appearance of a bunch of washers held tightly together. Each of the "washers" adds exactly five minutes to the timer. Placing his fingers on two, he rotates them away from him and then pulls the device from both ends until it clicks. He knows that all he has to do is depress the button-like end of the S.D.B.B.-1 and the timer will start.

Hearing Rosa's approach, he waits for her thumbs-up before starting the timer. Her thumbs-up is the first thing to come into view as she silhouettes in the door-way. Pushing the button end, he then places the device on the shelves holding the cleaners and moves quickly through the doorway.

Rosa, in just as much of a hurry, is already opening the door that goes to the barn trap door when he exits the room. They are both up and through the trap door in an instant and find their way to the same door they used before to enter the barn.

Pausing just for a second to listen, they hear nothing. Opening the door, they have a straight line of site to the gate they entered the compound through. Knowing they wouldn't stop even if they are noticed at this point, they make a beeline for it. Hurrying as much as possible, they are through the gate and headed up the hill at double time.

In her hurry, Rosa sends a rock rolling down the hill towards Charles. He dodges it skillfully without slowing down.

She curses herself, not because she almost hit Charles, but because anyone possibly observing would notice, and that was detrimental to their plan. She slows down a bit, to a more reasonable, safe, and quiet pace. Gaining control of her adrenaline, she knows they have plenty of time to reach their prior OP before the show starts.

Charles and Rosa are sitting in their previous position regaining their breath when the show starts. First is a distinct, not so subtle, *whoomp* noise from below the ground, then a couple more. Almost simultaneously, the farmhouse is lifted off the ground where it hovers for about a second or two before the bottom half is ripped upward and outward. Again, the remaining parts seem to hover for a second or two before sinking below ground. Almost as an afterthought, there is some commotion in the barn and the side farthest from the house explodes, leaving a gaping hole where the corner of the barn used to be. The strangest ripping and creaking sound ensues, giving warning to a partial impending collapse, which it does without any further hesitations.

The entire area is expelling dust and billowing it outwards in all directions, sharing it indiscriminately.

A guard exits the still clean and standing garage before the dust cloud reaches it. Running straight through the dust cloud, he hurries to see what is going on. Emerging from the outward billowing chaos just in time, he comes to a screeching halt on the edge of the pit where the farmhouse stood a moment ago.

From above, Rosa can see a fire developing in the crater containing the remains of the lab and farmhouse. She sees the remaining living being standing on the edge, scratching his head. Their side mission has been a success; their evidence is removed and any remaining bodies will be unidentifiable without extensive DNA testing, assuming any DNA can be found in the first place. Any of their possible DNA had been dealt with and standing on the edge of all their handiwork is their storyteller. He is the one who will sell their set up story about some kind of strange explosion, an explosion that destroyed all the scientists' work, and the scientists, and some guards along with it. Their job here was done. It is time to rejoin the others and wait for their trip home.

Feeling satisfied at a job well done, the two Trippers head back towards the temporary base camp and the rest of their team.

CHAPTER TWENTY ONE

At the end of an uneventful trip back to their base, Grey pulls up to their home for the mission and helps unload all people and contents before driving the van off to be hidden in a nearby barn.

Walking back to their shack, he contemplates the mission thus far. All have done well, and big picture-wise the mission is an extreme success. Pending Rosa and Charles' arrival, all of his Trippers have completed their parts pretty much unscathed. Only Mackenzie showed some wear and tear.

His thoughts go to the cherry gifts. With Miokel's story, Mackenzie's had become obvious. He even has a good idea what John's will be, but has yet to come up with a good idea for June. Perhaps he will have to ask Rosa's perspective when she returns; she might have some good

insight for him.

Entering the barn, Grey takes inventory of the situation. John is sitting with the scientists on the bales of straw in the back. They seem to have struck up a conversation, a good sign in this situation. June and Mackenzie sit off to one side together and are engaged in conversation. Off in a darker corner, Miokel sits on the ground with his back against the wall. He appears to be napping. Deciding to join him, Grey sits against the sliding door, near the man door and lowers his chin against his chest for a much-needed nap. Five minutes is all he needs to ramp up and finish the mission.

CHAPTER TWENTY TWO

As soon as they enter the barn, John shows the scientists to the rear of the structure, where they could sit on the bales with relative ease. He knew he would catch hell if he unties them, but thought water and food would be a good idea.

Gathering up energy bars and some water, he brings the loot to them to share.

Then, instead of walking away, he chooses to sit with them.

Having been crowded in the back of the van on a bumpy dirt road, they all got more acquainted than they probably would've liked. You can tell a lot about people in those situations; do they get mad when you are bounced into their space or do they laugh in humor or do they instead sit strong, or maybe try to help you stay in your space with a firm arm or bracing for you. These four: the three scientists and John, instinctually

were in it together, a little bit of smiles at the awkward moments, lots of bouncing off each other with only positive responses all around. It was obvious John is of similar nature to the lab rats.

Once they all settle in, John offers an apology of sorts, "Sorry about the rough removal guys."

A brief look of annoyance crosses each of their faces. Apparently, they had kinda forgot about that part already.

One of the scientists mumbles out while eating, "Yah, whats up with that?!"

Professor Nowak, his mouth completely full of food and water, just kind of nods in agreement and points to the scientists as if to say, "what he said."

"Not sure, to be honest; this is my first job." John replies.

Professor Nowak looks at him inquisitively, his mouth still working the food, "Can you explain who you are and who you represent?" Pausing to swallow his mouthful, "It would be great to know what is next and who I will be dealing with!" He suddenly looks very concerned.

John replies, "Not really, even if I were allowed to, it would be difficult to explain. I haven't quite figured out what I am going to say on third date disclosure yet."

The scientists look at him inquisitively again . . .

John continues, trying to give them some kind of answer, they seem like good people after all. "Maybe when we get where we are going the PABs will explain.

Until then, let's just say I was hand-picked because of my natural tendencies to thrive outside the norm. The way normal people live is just beyond me, I don't know how they do the drone, drone, drone, way of life. They find comfort in complete normalcy and routine, while I drown in it. This is the perfect gig for me, I've already figured out every day and every mission is going to be different. I'm going to thrive on it, I can tell.

"Not really an answer, so how about we go off topic. How about you sir? What makes you thrive?" John asks the lead scientist, hoping to crack him open a bit.

Smiling he can't help but answer, "My work, the research, the possibilities it brings. I would love to be the one who solves world hunger." Grinning ear to ear, "Imagine being able to fly over Africa dropping packets of seeds to all the villages, or somewhere it is so barren they fight over the least bit of water and food; drop each and every one of them drought-tolerant seeds with which to sustain themselves. Half of the violence in the world is over resources; imagine if that fight is taken away!"

John thinks for a bit, "What about collapse? Wouldn't that just lead to societal collapse? The whole foundation of the world I lived in is commercialism. All people working to produce income to fill those basic needs, if all the sudden no one needs to produce income for those basic needs, they would work less, or be able to at least.

All the big farms and supermarkets would die away. Entire communities of growers, harvesters, transporters etc. would be out of jobs. What would they do?"

Professor Nowak sighs, "Go home and grow their own crops, I hope! Yes it may lead to the end of the current system, but the current system is not that old, only about 60 years or so. . .before the 1940s, there were hardly any grocery stores, if you can imagine that! Not working to produce money for food would allow a simpler life, if one so desires. Or, at the very least, put the power back in the hands of the people. If you could grow food anywhere, then you could live anywhere."

One of the assistants chimes in, "It might be the end of GMOs as well. They are created to help the mega farms keep up with demand. If demand goes down or disappears, then there is no reason to grow a lesser quality food. Heck! They may even be forced to raise the quality of their product in order to keep any business at all," he says.

John, unsure of what he means, "I don't get that statement." Being of a time when all foods are super processed and don't even look like food anymore, John is unsure of where the scientists are going with all this. In 2054 when he is from, he simply puts a food pill in his mouth in the morning. Who has time to cook anyway, he has to go to work in order to . . . "Ah, I get it now." John nods his head, suddenly realizing the changes Professor Nowak's

technology could bring.

The other scientist pipes in, "Tell him your biggest fear, sir."

Dr. Nowak obliges his assistant, "The obvious one, the one that may be coming into fruition right now! Someone of greed stealing the research, and either destroying it or using it to extend their control and therefore expand their bank account while preventing others from doing the same."

"No, I meant the other one," the other scientist says, smirking at his boss.

Professor Nowak laughing, "Oh yah, that one wasn't prominent on my mind right now." Pointing at John, "Kind of like what you said, uh . . ." searching for his name.

Not sure if he had provided his name, probably not, John extends his hand to shake the lead scientist's hand, "John, my name is John."

With just a moment's hesitation Professor Nowak extends his hand as well. "Nowak, Professor Nowak. Good to meet you, John."

The Professor continues, "Yes, my biggest fear is that during the collapse of the current way of being, instead of society turning towards progress and self-sufficiency, society instead turns into a world of chaos, that out of fear because of loss of work or whatever, people turn against each other instead of learning the lessons to become self-sufficient again."

The assistant adds, "But instead of succumbing to his fear, the professor did what he had to do to protect the research, and we all were working on a plan to help the world transition into a new way of being. For, to quote, 'fear is the mind killer,' after all."

John looks at him, not getting the reference.

All three scientists look at him aghast. "What?!" they say, almost in unison.

The other assistant pipes in again, "You mean you haven't read *Dune*? Someone like you, really? I mean, it seems up your alley."

Professor Nowak says to the quiet scientist, "Go ahead, you seem to have it in your mind the best."

The quiet scientist blushes and hesitates for a second, obviously not used to being on stage. He steps through his normal meek and mild nature to do the quote justice.

He begins, "I must not fear. Fear is the mind-killer. Fear is the little-death that brings total obliteration. I will face my fear. I will permit it to pass over me and through me. And when it has gone past I will turn the inner eye to see its path. Where the fear has gone there will be nothing. Only I will remain."

"Wow!" John exclaims. "That is great . . . and so true. I'm going to have to read this *Dune* tale."

The scientists moving on from their resistance suddenly come alive with passion as they discuss their

research and other geekdom stuff with John.

Shortly, it becomes quite apparent to John why they had hired mercenaries to guard them and their research. The lead scientist said it best, "We have created a never-ending seed. Once you have planted the seed, it will grow continuously forever. Adapting to the different seasons of that environment or almost any environment, it will produce that fruit or vegetable for as long as it is planted there, without expanding." The power in that tiny little seed is way beyond its volume. A seed so small, the wind could remove it from your hand, still has the power to change to world. One little seed planted changes everything over time.

John wonders how to explain even to a scientist that he is from 2054 but that they actually came to 2014 from 2114; this is beyond him at this moment. Mostly, John wants to tell the scientists that he is wondering why being from the future, he isn't aware of this world-changing technology. This is the kind of thing that saves humans from hunger. No-one would have to rely on the system or corporations to provide for them. Once they had the seeds in hand, anybody would be able to feed their family for life with no reliance on any system or government.

John's thoughts are interrupted by Grey, "Ok it is time, get them ready." he says.

Knowing what comes next, John wonders what it

will be like for the scientists to time travel. Talk about a journey of a lifetime!

He also wonders if any of the three will die (albeit temporarily) from the journey. He personally is hoping he got his 'death' out of the way on his first trip, as though it only happens once. One can hope. Or at the very least, like the bingo games of lore, where all the numbered balls are placed inside a giant spinning cage and each Tripper has an assigned number and only when that numbered ball is drawn from the cage will it be their turn for the heart to stop. He also hopes there are about a million numbers . . .

Standing up and thanking the scientists for the conversation, he saunters over to Grey, "Did you know these guys have created a never-ending seed of sorts? It would enable self-sufficiency to almost anyone and everyone!"

Grey looks at John sternly, "I did not and neither do you."

"But what about the life-changing technology, what happens to it? I'm from about 40 years from now and have no idea this technology exists. Of course, I know we are taking it to . . ."

"2114," Grey helps him out.

"Right, so do I not know about it because we grabbed it before my time frame? Or what!"

Grey puts his arm around John's shoulder, more to stop his talking and thoughts than as a comforting move.

"It is a mind fuck, isn't it." smirking he continues, "It's best not to think too much; it can get confusing. Focus on the task at hand, don't overthink and you will be fine. You did great today by the way, keep it up!" Squeezing John a little tighter, he then lets him go.

Grey addresses all, "Ok, saddle up, it is time to go."

John wanders off a bit to gather his gear. Not think?! Does he know who he's talking to here . . .

Grey walks away from John and steps outside to see if Charles and Rosa have arrived. Having just been informed by Miokel, who he had sent out on watch as soon as he awoke from his catnap, that they were approaching, he is itching to hear how their side mission went.

He walks out just in time to see them arrive.

"How did it go?" Grey asks, all business as usual.

Rosa smiles at him, "It was great!"

Grey laughs, "Good, glad it went well."

"Yes sir." Charles puts out his hand to him, "All science apparently destroyed. One witness left to sell the story, just as we wanted."

Grey takes his hand and by giving it a quick squeeze, expresses his gratitude, "Awesome. Thanks, Charles."

Then, addressing Rosa, "And you! How was it for you?" They put their arms around each other as a brother and sister would.

"Awesome," is her enthusiastic reply, "you should've

seen the explosion, it was awesome! The whole house lifted and then sank below ground, it was awesome!"

Grey just grins ear to ear. Her joy is astounding.

"Ok good, glad it was . . . what was that word again?"

Pulling away from Grey she applies a well directed, precise, heart punch to his chest. "Awesome. The word is awesome." She smiles at him.

Grey centers himself just a bit, even he is open to a little joy, but the time for the trip home is approaching rapidly. He looks at an imaginary watch on his arm, "Ok, our ride will be here soon, we need to be in the ready."

High on success and adrenaline, they continue to ham it up as they enter the barn for the last time. It is time to take the show back home.

CHAPTER
TWENTY THREE

John opens his eyes . . . instantly grateful, for he is alive and breathing. And he wasn't even looking at Charles' ugly mug, even better! As he looks around, he sees that all seven team members are fine and breathing, none of them had failed to return from the tripping dead this time.

Half-expecting to see the three scientists, he is surprised they are not here. They tripped only seconds before the seven team members, yet they are no where to be seen. John was so looking forward to seeing their scientist minds react to the trip through time—would they even realize upon arrival that they had time-traveled or would they just think they had teleported, a feat in its self in their time?

His rambling thoughts continue as he gathers himself. John has vague memories of coming backward out of a

sideways tornado. Remembering yesterday's trip into a mosaic swirl of images before the shocking wake-up by Charles, he supposes this is possible. Looking over his shoulder, he spots the lookout window of the control room above him in the wall. Yep, apparently they go forward when going back in time, and return to the present backward. "There's something ironic about that." He says to himself.

"You coming?" He hears Rosa's voice above him.

Looking up, he sees her outstretched hand. Taking her offer of assistance, he uses her help to gather himself to his feet. Surprised at her strength, he pulls a little bit on her arm, receiving an instant pull back from her as he is lifted to his feet. Her strength surpasses his for sure. He will have to keep that in mind when he hits on her . . . perhaps she will want to be on top.

"Thanks, Rosa. I like a strong woman!"

"Whatever," she replies in return, smiling the whole time. Starting to figure him out, she gathers she will just have to treat him like an immature soldier who is learning she is not "just a woman." Having been there before, she revels on the process.

On his feet, John looks around the T.R.M. for the cases, they are nowhere to be found. Wondering if they are in the same place as the scientists, he poses the question to Rosa.

CHAPTER TWENTY THREE

"The cases and the scientists?" John asks of her.

"The PABs have them for sure. It's pretty standard for us to only return with our original 7. I think all retrievals are sent elsewhere, and always sent back just before us. This way, if something goes wrong, we will still be there to handle it, instead of traveling again." She points her thumb over her shoulder towards the wall that isn't really a wall. He can't help but stare at it. "Don't worry, if we forgot something we will be the first to know!" She winks at John and starts walking towards the exit, the door they entered through just yesterday, albeit a life time ago.

As he starts walking, John wonders if he is the only one that feels like he has been hit by a truck.

Looking around he sees Grey, Miokel and Charles are already through the exit door, maybe even through the next set of doors as well, wherever they are, Rosa is quickly catching up to them for sure.

He notices the other two newbies are hesitating a bit. Mackenzie, holding her arm close to her belly in its sling, pauses to look up, and June is scanning around the room as well. Seemingly noticing the viewing window for the first time, June looks up at it, frozen in time.

"Thanks for waiting!" John calls out to them as he is finally able to convince his legs to walk. He heads towards the door.

They also seem to suddenly be unable to leave the

T.R.M. They all seem reluctant, like perhaps they are afraid they will never return and are taking one last look just in case.

"We will be back," John assures them. "I'm starving. Lets go eat!" Putting an arm around each of them he starts walking, ushering them towards the door, ignoring his owns doubts.

The three newbies catch up to the senior team members shortly after they go through the first set of swinging doors. In fact, they are standing there waiting for them. Seeing them, Grey suddenly starts clapping. Instantly the other senior members of the team join him in applauding the rookies. Mackenzie, June and John all seem to blush simultaneously. None of them are really used to positive reinforcement.

Rosa gives out a, "Good job rooks!"

Mackenzie finds herself looking at the floor. Miokel calls her out on it, "Put your head up rookie, you ALL did great!" Blushing more, she manages to raise her head, still feeling shame. She manages to make eye contact with the senior Trippers. Its only then that she notices, even Charles is smiling and clapping . . . even for her.

When it lets up, Grey addresses Miokel, "I have to go see the new brass. Let's catch up later."

"Sounds good, Boss. Good luck with the Colonel, can't wait to hear about him." Winking at Grey, he turns to the

other team members, "Come on, let's hit the showers."

John asks him, "Do we eat first?"

"Absolutely!" Miokel replies.

Grey stands there and watches as his team walks through the other set of swinging doors. As June walks by Grey, she looks up at him with gratitude in her eyes. She is grateful to have a leader such as him. Hoping to always have him nearby, she starts to say so and instead breaks eye contact and walks away, not sure of how he would react to such a statement from her.

After they go through the swinging doors, he stands there, still listening. Coming from the other set of doors he can hear the hum of the machine winding down. As the last team members' footsteps fade away to silence, all he can hear is the gentle hum of machinery. Now the comforting sound of home; he has spent so many years living here, underground, listening to the manmade sounds that accompany life in a secure structure filled with computers and machinery. With all the air and water pumped in, and all the waste pumped out there is not a time of day vacant of mechanical noise. The only place that has a semblance of silence is his apartment. There and there only is he in control of the noise; and the sooner he talks to the new CO, the sooner he can get to his quiet zone.

Grey walks off, pushing through the swinging doors, and heads down the hall, leaving only the sound of doors swinging behind, he takes his footsteps with him.

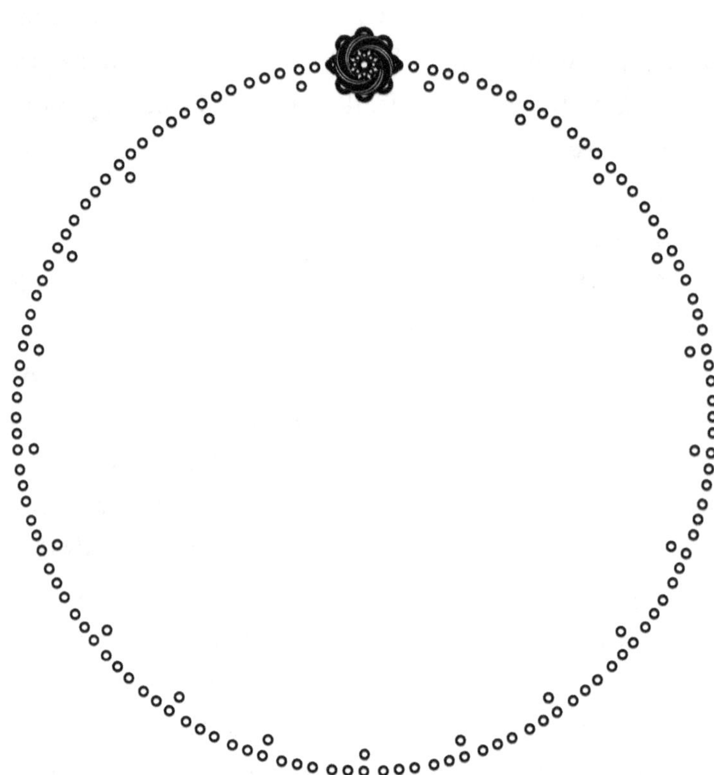

CHAPTER TWENTY FOUR

The Colonel sits in his small private office of the climate-and-spy-controlled kind. No one has access to what goes on in here except the Colonel himself. The recordings taken from the cameras in this office are for his eyes only; no backups, no copies.

Speaking of tapes, Colonel Petzer is watching a tape of the infamous incident with the big Cajun guy who lost it while heading out on a mission. Mr. Roberts had obviously lied to him. The team did try to stop the man from hurting himself and wrecking the place, but they did not team up against the security guards to protect the giant of a man. And once he went totally off the deep end, they were in fact crucial in stopping him. It was obvious that security would not have been able to subdue him without their help.

Colonel Petzer stops the playback and contemplates what he just watched.

There is a knock on the door.

"Come in."

His assistant says, "Grey's team is back."

"Thank you."

The door closes.

Good, I want to talk to a couple of those guys about this, he thinks. The recorded incident doesn't jive at all with the story Mr. Roberts fed him and he wants to get to the bottom of it quick! He doesn't like the taste of bullshit.

A short time later, the assistant again opens the door, "James Grey is here, sir."

"Ok, see him in."

Grey enters the office. Looking up, Colonel Petzer notices he is sweaty, dirty and still in his tripper suit. This is the Colonel's first close-up of one of their suits. He was told about the technology but has yet to experience it. In this natural state it doesn't look like much: layers of fabric attached to a mechanized coverall is what it looks like initially. The fabric is attached in such a way as to allow access to the items located below while keeping them mostly out of sight.

"Is it true that your jumpsuit changes appearance?" He asks.

Grey smirks, remembering how new the Colonel is to

this unit, "Absolutely, sir. There are some programmed outfits, for lack of a better term, or I can change it consciously based on real-time situations. It's all an illusion of sorts, sir, and to be honest, a tech could better explain it all. A hologram might be a better word to use than illusion, even."

Colonel Petzer smiles, "I will certainly ask a technician. Mostly I want to see it change. Is there a way you can turn it into a nice, shiny new uniform, the kind you would stand before your new commanding officer in?"

Grey almost blushes, "Absolutely sir, will that be a requirement from here on in?"

"No it will not be a requirement, not after a . . . trip would you call it?" Colonel Petzer asks.

"Trip or mission, sir." Grey answers.

"Great, thank you." Colonel Petzer responds.

Colonel Petzer watches the suit miraculously change into a uniform much like the one he is currently wearing. Pretty identical in fact, just a few differences in service ribbons and with Grey on the name tag instead of Petzer. Looking Grey up and down he notices that Grey still shows the wear and tear of his mission, but the uniform looks to be in impeccable shape. Obviously the suit only has control over itself and not the appearance of the person wearing it, so the tripper will have to change his personal appearance to match the suit's 'outfit.' He also notices the layers of fabric are no longer noticeable either. The effect of the

hologram does indeed hide the items hidden underneath: guns, knives, other tools, anything that fits can be concealed below. Any futuristic technology they might need to carry will be hidden from ancient eyes until revealed, a handy thing indeed. In his mind, he wonders how it would fare during a pat down, a question for later. He does manage to notice details of the disguise that would never pass his inspection. He will have to put some of the new funding into expanding the technology of the suits so the Trippers will have a better chance of surviving a critical inspection by an experienced eye such as his own.

The Colonel looks up at Grey, "I will be looking to you senior men to help me transition, to give me beta and other inside information as to what has and hasn't worked here in the past. Obviously, being from outside this project, I have no inclination as to who and what has brought us to this point, our successes and failures. Can I count on you for that?"

"Absolutely, sir. I'm happy to assist in the continued success of our missions and this project, sir." Pausing, "It's way better than retirement."

Laughing the Colonel responds, "Absolutely, I agree." Reaching into his desk drawer he retrieves the bottle he found rolling around in the back and pours some in a small glass, also retrieved from the drawer, "Drink?"

A firm believer in celebrating success, Grey reaches

for the small glass, "Thank you sir."

Colonel Petzer continues, "I, of course, would like a debrief of how your mission went. But honestly I am more intrigued by something else." Grey waits for it, "Now, tell me about the Cajun. There seems to be a couple of different versions surrounding the incident; tell me what really happened."

Grey gives him his version of the events, true as his memory allows.

Having just watched the video, the incident is fresh in the Colonel's mind. He notes just a couple small differences between what he just watched and Grey's telling of the story, all could be attributed to the mind altering the memories, which it does over time for some reason, or personal perspective even. Seven people involved in an incident or on an adventure, will have seven different experiences, and therefore seven different stories. Before they talk to each other at least, then and only then would they totally jive with each other's perspective of the incident. A key give away to pre-rehearsed incident reporting for sure. He ran across this once or twice over the years with his troopers, usually covering each other's ass and sometimes, something worse than that.

Bantering back and forth, the Colonel eventually asks Grey what caused the whole thing.

"Um, hard to say, sir. The PABs had him on calming drugs to make sure he didn't go berserk during the training process. We weaned him off them during the last couple days before mission go; maybe it was that or maybe he would've anyway. I think, sir, if we had just kept him drug free it wouldn't have been as much of a shock." Shrugging his shoulders, "But who knows, he was a berserker anyway, that's why we chose him."

"Ok," is Colonel Petzer's only response.

"Just to add," Grey decides to offer his opinion if for no reason other than testing the waters, "We ended up paying off the two goons in the end. Perhaps that would've been the smarter approach to begin with. Might isn't always the best answer to a problem."

"Well put, James" the Colonel acknowledges Grey's train of thought.

The use of Grey's first name catches him off guard a bit and the Colonel notices. "Did I get it wrong, your name?"

Grey smiling replied, "No sir, I just don't hear it very much, most just call me Grey. James it is sir, just in private if you would?"

"Sure thing."

Having it handy, the Colonel takes another look at Grey's file; amongst other things, it contains a timeline of his duty time, missions, leave etc. He notices (at least in the first couple pages of the timeline) that Grey has spent all his leave time right here in the compound.

"When's the last time you went up top? It says here you spend all your leave down here."

Grey answers, "Never been up top. I find it best to stay in our world down here. I just put the vacation package in my entertainment center and off I go for a day or two."

Colonel Petzer asks, "So you have no idea what current life is like?"

"Just mine, sir. Nothing about up top. How about you?"

"Yes, I just came down from up there. This world is new to me, your world. It will be an adjustment for me. I, however, will not have the luxury of staying below. I will have to go top side from time to time to meet with the PAB's, and keep funding flowing our way. You know, political stuff like that." He gives Grey a knowing wink.

Chuckling, Grey replies, "Yes, sir, you can have that world. I prefer this one. I love working with the Trippers and especially breaking in the new ones."

Curious about something, the Colonel asked Grey, "Ever think about retirement? I mean based on what you just said, I'm guessing no."

"You guessed right, sir. I have no need to retire. I am loving life and, as far as I can tell, am still excelling at my job."

"I would say you are James Grey. You are indeed excelling at your job. Your record jacket supports that statement, and I can tell just from our short conversation and from reading your file, that you are a key part of this

program." The Colonel pauses for a second, "The seed I want to plant with you today is about switching over to training at some point. I don't mean training your new team members but training new Trippers. The 'boot camp' side of things. If the funding I am told about is coming our way, we are ripe for expansion, and there will be a need to expand our training facilities. You would be a great man to be involved in setting the tone during that expansion."

"I appreciate the offer, sir. I'm just not ready for even that form of retirement." Laughing, Grey continues, "I am having too much fun. I have a great, well-rounded team, even with three FNG's." He waits for the Colonel's reaction to the term and gets no negative reaction. "I also have a hard time believing I can be happy just being in one place all the time. After years of time traveling for a living it would be hard to transition to just being here."

"Yes, that makes sense. I just have to say that with increased funding we will be able to send your recruits on trips BEFORE sending them on a mission. You might be a perfect Tripper to help them through that learning curve."

"That is an increase in funding, and would be extremely helpful! Even though things rarely go wrong during the trips, it would be beneficial to experience the feeling of time travel before the added pressure of a first mission." Grey said in agreement.

"I'll leave it for now, but, like I said, seed planted."

CHAPTER
TWENTY FIVE

Leaving Grey behind to see the new boss, the rest of the team heads towards their ready room. Unknown to the newbies, the room is full of beer, coffee, and a buffet of the team's favorite foods.

Miokel leads the team towards their reward. As he does, his stomach growls in anticipation, it knows he will soon fill it with gratuitous amounts of meat lasagna, and ranch dressing-covered salad. Not sure when its owner first introduced the luscious meal to its diet, but gracious just the same that it has become his favorite post-trip recovery food.

Using the thunderous sound as an opening, John catches up to the usually, mostly silent, second in charge, "What was that? Did you capture a tiger in there?"

Miokel laughs, smiles even.

"I'm usually really hungry after a mission. I don't eat much before one, sometimes for days," he trails off in thought. John waits for him to return. He doesn't.

John says to Miokel, "Now what? What happens next? Do we go out tomorrow? Are they bringing in whores and booze to help us unwind from this or what?"

John's unabated enthusiasm has Miokel laughing, "Not quite! We will have a couple days off, and then they will more than likely assign us a new mission, if not, we train until they do."

John asks, "How often can I expect to travel through time?"

"Frequently and often my friend!"

"Great! Here's to hoping I don't die EVERY time." Chuckling and walking, John sincerely hopes every mission goes as well as this one; all things considered, this one was a cake walk, except for dying of course. Regardless, he is very happy at his new lot in life. Lots of fun, adventure and opportunities to play with electronics and problem solve. Now if he could only figure out how to get laid in this new world. He glances over at Mackenzie walking nearby.

The team arrives at their ready room. Reaching the door first, Miokel opens it and holds it for the entire crew, well, except for Grey and Mackenzie that is. Grey is off meeting with the new boss. Having only worked under the thumb of the previous guy, Miokel wonders what changes are imminent and how the managerial change will affect him and his duties. He hopes minimally.

And Mackenzie's location? Miokel had swung the whole crew by the medical center to drop her off there. He figured she deserved it and it sent a message to the entire crew about the value of the team. We are in this together, is always Miokel's message.

He is about to enter and close the door when he hears a familiar walk coming down the hall. Being of that sort, he has already learned the gaits of the new guys and he recognizes Mackenzie's purposeful stride while she was still a ways down the hall. He will wait right here for her.

His thoughts wander to the speed of modern body repair, he knows from experience it took them approximately a minute to place all her broken and dislocated hand parts to their previous locations and about another minute to spray on a protective covering. The spray cast not only protects the area from banging and normal use, it also contains repairing agents that speed the body's normal repair process. In just three days, Mackenzie will have to return to the medical center to have the patch removed; her hand will be completely healed.

The sounds of her rounding the corner remove him from his thoughts and he focuses on her as she develops a smile when she sees him holding the door for her.

The smile comes a little from the pain meds, but mostly from the act of chivalry Mackenzie is experiencing. Something her ex would never do, and this guy was just one of her work partners. Well not 'just;' it is becoming obvious to her that they are in it together and this team has to be tight in order to accomplish their missions. The stakes are a lot higher than making the international playoffs with her professional soccer team. There are life and death, not to mention world-changing consequences attached to this team's actions. . .and she loves it!

"Thank you, sir!" she smiles at her teammate.

"Absolutely, m'lady. I'm glad you made it to your welcome home party!" he smiles back at her, "What food did you ask for?"

"Bangers and mash and Turkey tetrazzini were the two things I asked for. Strange combination, I know." Sheepish, she looks at him.

Miokel shrugs his shoulders, "I ask for lasagna and ranch dressing, and I am Ottoman. Nothing to do with lineage. Just kick-ass recovery food."

"Recovery food and comfort food is what I went for. I got hooked on bangers and mash while traveling with the league, and turkey tetrazzini is my favorite Thanksgiving leftover meal. It's comfort food for me," she says.

"Great!" he says, "Now get in there and eat a bunch

of it!" he helps her through, placing his hand on her back and pushing gently.

After she walks in, he looks up and down the hall for Grey. He doesn't spot him. Or hear him. Knowing he may be a little longer with the new boss he decides to close the door and get the team eating. He will have to encourage Rosa and Charles to do so; it is their custom to all eat together, but this time there will be an exception to the rule. He enters and closes the door behind him.

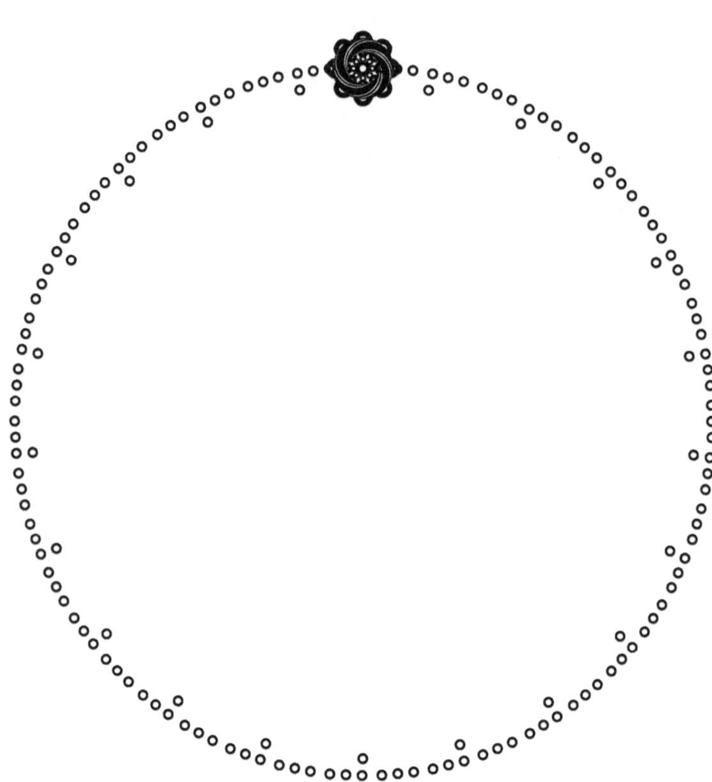

CHAPTER
TWENTY SIX

Grey arrives when his team is about halfway through their meals. All look up as the door opens; seeing who it is, a cheer goes about the room.

Smiling at the greeting, he places a backpack on his chair, and picks up a plate from the buffet along the wall. Filling his plate full, a little of everything, he grabs his seat at the end of the table, placing the pack on the floor.

"Did I miss anything exciting?" he asks.

Rosa pipes up, "Not a thing, we have done nothing but feed our faces."

She, of the military variety, finished her meal of southern fried chicken about five minutes after she sat down and has spent the last 10 minutes chilling and watching her teammates' eating rituals. A lot can be learned from that she thinks; do they just consume it as all business like she just did, or do they savor it and enjoy it like Charles does. June seems to be in the latter category as well and John; well, John is John. He is doing more talking than eating. It's amazing to her that a computer geek like him is so talkative.

Smiling, Grey simply says, "Good, best first thing to do after a mission. Glad you all are training the newbies right." Grey continues, "Sorry I am late, won't happen again." he looks at Charles and Rosa specifically.

"We have new Brass we report to and I had to go meet him. As first meetings go, it went very well. He has a good grasp on what we are all about and he, Colonel Petzer, comes with increased funding, which is a good thing. It appears this division is about to grow and expand and you will be a part of it."

Charles speaks, "What exactly does that mean? More rules and regulations probably . . ." he grabs at his pocket absentmindedly. "That would be a mistake I think."

"That would be bullshit!" Rosa adds.

"I agree" Grey continues, "it would be—we'll go with—a mistake." Smiling at Rosa, she blushes slightly.

Miokel chimes in, "I like bullshit, personally. If they try to make us all prim and proper, tighten the constraints, change who we are, it won't work. Do they think that rule followers and normal people can do what we do? A conformist could never go back in time and change . . ."

CHAPTER TWENTY SIX

Grey puts a hand on his shoulder.

John tips back his chair in order to view Miokel around June, who is sitting between them in her usual spot. For two of the newbies, this is the first show of emotion they have seen from the stone-faced man. Mackenzie, however, is starting to realize the amount of passion Miokel has hidden within that stone exterior; his depth of professionalism subdues a lot of his natural personality. She relates to that immensely.

Looking Miokel in the eye, Grey continues, "Colonel Petzer agrees." He shakes Miokel's shoulder a little bit with his hand, "He totally agrees. I can tell already from just our initial conversation. It's obvious he is as passion-ate as you are," he looks around the table, "as passionate as we all are, about what we do. He is on the side of his field personnel, that is blatantly obvious. The Colonel has been in charge of field personnel or special units, for most of his career; he thrives on it, it seems. Which is—"

"Perfect." Charles finishes Grey's sentence, unknow-ingly removing the protective hand from the meds he had no idea he was protecting.

"At this point, are there any questions?" Grey asks, the question directed more towards the rookies.

Without hesitation John responds, "Yes! I have tons of questions, where do I start?" he asks himself rhetorically.

"Get used to not having most of them answered."

Grey quips before John could continue.

Laughter erupts from around the table. Except for John, of course, John looks hurt.

Seeing this, Grey addresses it, "We will have a rookie meeting on the morning of the 6th day at 9:00 a.m. You, Mackenzie and June will all need to be in attendance; we can address all the newbie questions at that time. Which reminds me actually—"

Grey dabs at his face with a cloth napkin and looks at June, "All rooks to the front of the room." June looks surprised, eyes going wide, what is happening?

"Seriously, all of you, John and Mackenzie as well."

For a moment all you can hear are chairs scooting on the ground and the shuffling of feet.

Charles and Rosa start chanting, "fng's, fng's" quietly at first, then louder, "Fng's, Fng's, Fng's" until they are chanting pretty loudly, they slow it down a bit "FNG's, FNG's . . ."

Miokel helps Grey assemble the three newbies in front of the buffet table, then joins the rest of the team who are lining up facing them.

Grey stands in between, facing the new members of his team. Without looking behind him, he motions with his hand for the chanting to stop.

Rosa does the popping cherry sound as a finale to their chanting. Loudly, it reverberates across the room enticing nervous smiles of relief from the three brand new Trippers lined up in front of the buffet table.

Grey speaks his piece, "You have presented your-selves well. We can see that they have chosen wisely. . .grateful to have you on our team, we are presenting you with a sign of appreciation."

Leaning back a bit, Grey puts out his hand, into which Miokel places an object.

Addressing Mackenzie, "Put out your hand." she obliges and in it he places a small object made of high tech materials, with a currently unknown purpose.

"This neat little mechanism attaches to the sleeve of your tripper suit. It has a sensor capable of reading your bio-rhythms and thoughts." He lets that sink in a bit with a dramatic pause, "When you tell it to, it will dispense a lock pick or handcuff master key into your hand, again at your discretion. It will take some practice." he winks at her, "Your wrists and hands will be eternally grateful for this gift from now until you are old and the arthritis kicks in." He nods towards her damaged hand, "You will no longer need to disassemble an appendage to help a team member out." There are a few chuckles in the room. "Your extreme dedication to helping out a fellow Tripper has been noticed!"

Grey sidesteps over to John and makes eye contact with him.

"We couldn't help but notice your inappropriate relationship with computers," genuine laugher abounds in the room, "Being of the inappropriate sort we decided to encourage this behavior." He reaches behind him and Miokel puts a bigger object in his hand this time. Bringing it around, Grey places in John's hands, a picture book of computers and their designs through time, what was once known as a coffee table book. This book was created for the computer lover in mind. It has detailed beta and coffee table book size pictures to admire and drool over. From their warehouse sized brethren of the 1970s to the scary small and smart computers of the 2070s, the book bears the title, *100 Years of Computers, A Photo Tribute*.

John looks at the book in amazement. Even in his time frame of sixty years ago, print books were a thing of the past. How did Grey do it? How did he come up with it in such a short notice. Grey in fact, had to call in an owed favor from one of the geek supervisors. He was owed the favor for playing a heavy for him during a small crisis. John grins in gratitude, somehow this low-tech gift is perfect for this high-tech guy.

Grey moves over to June next.

"You are our persuader, as I call it. I think you referred to yourself, or were referred to, as a grifter in your Bio; that has too many negative connotations to be used for someone like you." He smiles at her. She has been grinning

since he moved in front of her and continues it a little bigger. "People just want to do what you say and have your attention, even if they know it is just for a little while. One of your gifts is your look and your presence. Unlike John's gift, this one can travel with you." He hands her a small box. Opening it, June pulls out a gadget of sorts. Looking it over, she cannot tell what it is or what it is for.

Helping her out, Grey continues, "This is a mirror of the kind you would call Alien technology. It will attach to your biorhythms and thoughts just like Mackenzie's gift. With just the right thoughts you can make it appear before you." Putting his hands up to show her, he demonstrates how it works, "Either floating as a head sized mirror at face level or (looking down at his palm) a hand mirror that appears in your hand and can be moved with your hand like it truly exists as a tangible object." Amazingly the mirror appears and moves just as Grey willed it.

"We are by no means suggesting you look in the mirror a lot," Grey smirks, "Just that your presence is your greatest tool and if you should want to check your image, you will be able to do so on a mission."

From behind him, "Or look around a corner."

"Or signal somebody."

Twisting his head at her, "Exactly." Grey adds.

Stepping away from her, he stands next to Miokel, and assuming a military type pose he calls out, "Mac!

John! June!"

"For surviving and thriving on your first mission, we salute you."

All four of them slowly lift their right arms, very slowly, almost painfully slow, into a salute position and say in unison:

"The old you is dead."

Salute hands come down briskly and with purpose.

"As a Tripper, you thrive."

Grey smiles and releases from bearing; walking forward, he shakes hands with each new Tripper.

All senior members walk up and congratulate the new teams members. Hand shaking, congrats and accolades all around. If one were observing (as someone surely is), they would notice genuine greetings and acknowledgments amongst the team. It would be clear to them that this team is different; they are tight and seem to be made for each other. This team is new together and yet one would already think they have been working together for a very long time. It's almost as if they have done this together before.

Grey shouts out above the din of all six talking at once, "Ok! Lets wrap this up. Its time to call it . . . three of you know what that means. For the other three, you have five days off to do just about whatever you want. Be prepared to sleep a lot, time travel is a lot like jet lag, but worse. Other than that, explore your new world down here. I know you haven't really been free to do so until now. So, enjoy it!"

Excited and exhausted, no one argues with Grey, and they all gather their things and head for the door.

Getting to it first, Rosa chooses to hold the door for them all. Giving her thanks, they all proceed before her. As the last person walks out, she takes a good look around the room, making sure nothing important or anything anybody would want, is left behind. She knows from experience, this room will be spotless the next time they see it. All evidence of this mission will be removed and Grey will walk in, new one in hand.

She smiles because in just a few days she will get to do it again. She hopes, again and again and again . . .

"See you in five days, I'm gonna go read!" she puts out to the room as she turns off the light and closes the door behind her.

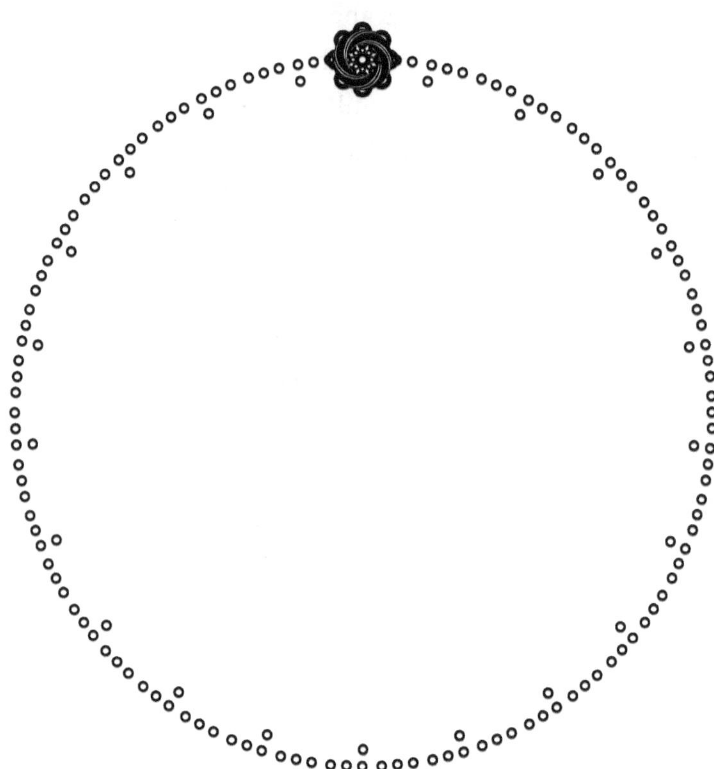

ABOUT THE AUTHOR

C.M. Halstead is a new and budding member of the author community. The stories coming out of his fingers are full of adventure and the characters called to it.

A wise man once said, ". . . we have to do what we have to do. And well, thats just the way it is . . ." One of the simplest and yet profound statements of all time. Have you ever resisted something you knew you were suppose to do? Something you were made for, something you were called to do even. I bet you've been thinking about it for years . . . . Well time to take action.

The resistance is gone, and it is an amazing ride. Come along with me as we journey through the soul of the writer in me. I look forward to sharing the stories and lessons of life through the characters and their endeavors.

Ps, did someone say bio? Ready for it: Husband, Dad, Marine for life, MKP brother, Explorer, Lover of the Outdoors and Teacher of Life to all that ask of it . . .